Kate Fortune's Journal Entry

Together at last! I've missed my whole family so much over the past months. It's nice to finally be able to share in their happiness. Many things have happened in their lives. Several weddings have taken place, many babies have been born and estranged couples reunited. I'm glad that some of my special gifts worked their magic and brought each child and grandchild love and joy. It's been a roller-coaster ride, but I wouldn't have missed it for all the world. I can't wait to see what the next fifty years bring!

A LETTER FROM THE AUTHOR

Dear Reader,

I was tantalized by the whole concept of our Fortune's Children series from the very beginning. We all had fun developing our different suspense and danger elements, but the heart of each story is linked to the Fortune family. Although the Fortunes amassed a giant financial dynasty, the true legacy they passed on to each other was wealth of a different kind. This is a family who knows what love is, and who sticks together through thick and thin.

The series ends with Rebecca's love story. She's not one to be impressed with champagne and a candlelit dinner. She wants babies. She wants a hearth and home. She learned the power of love from the nest of her own family, and there's no way she's willing to settle for less. Her hero despairs that she's a hopeless romantic...but I tend to see her as a hard-core realist. It takes a tough, strong cookie to fight for what really matters, and she believes in families.

Me too.

I hope you enjoy *The Baby Chase* and am enclosing my best wishes to you and all your families—

Jennifer Greene

The Baby Chase

JENNIFER GREENE

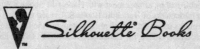

Silhouette Books

Published by Silhouette Books

America's Publisher of Contemporary Romance

To my fellow PT'ers...who else
would have put up with all the petunias?
Thanks from my heart for all the support.

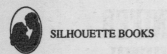 **SILHOUETTE BOOKS**

THE BABY CHASE

Copyright © 1997 by Harlequin Books S.A.

ISBN 0-373-50188-9

Special thanks and acknowledgment to Jennifer Greene
for her contribution to the Fortune's Children series.

Printed in U.S.A.

JENNIFER GREENE

Jennifer Greene's first book came out in 1983, and since then she has written forty-nine books in the romance genre. She has won numerous awards for her writing, including two RWA RITA Awards and both Career and Lifetime Achievement awards from *Romantic Times.*

Ms. Greene is from Michigan, where she lives with her husband and two children. Before writing full-time, she worked as a teacher, counselor and human-resources manager. Her background includes a degree in English and Psychology from Michigan State University, where she was honored as an outstanding woman graduate for the work she did for women on campus.

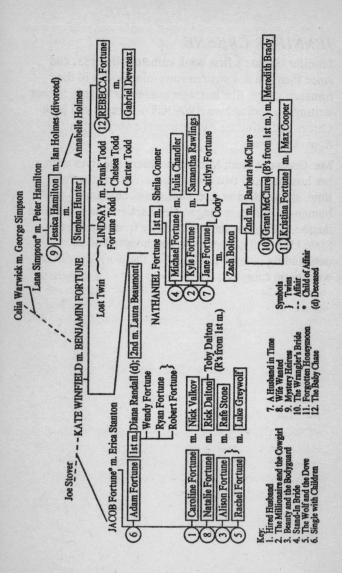

Key:
1. Hired Husband
2. The Millionaire and the Cowgirl
3. Beauty and the Bodyguard
4. Stand-In Bride
5. The Wolf and the Dove
6. Single with Children

7. A Husband in Time
8. Wife Wanted
9. Mystery Heiress
10. The Wrangler's Bride
11. Forgotten Honeymoon
12. The Baby Chase

Symbols

} Twins
--- Affair
* Child of Affair
(d) Deceased

F⦿RTUNE'S Children

Meet the Fortunes—three generations of a family with a legacy of wealth, influence and power. As they unite to face an unknown enemy, shocking family secrets are revealed...and passionate new romances are ignited.

REBECCA FORTUNE: The nurturing and loving author is still single, but she wants to be a mother. She's decided she will do anything to have a baby—even if she has to seduce the man who won't accept her for who she is....

GABRIEL DEVEREAX: The wary private detective doesn't believe in love or family. But after one steamy night of passion with Rebecca, he hadn't counted on what would happen next—he was about to become a father!

KATE FORTUNE: With the Fortunes reunited, matriarch Kate is encouraged by the fulfillment and happiness in her children's and grandchildren's lives. Is Kate destined for a romance of her own now that the family crisis is resolved?

STERLING FOSTER: Kate's attorney and closest confidante has stood by her through decades of family turmoil. Was it just professional loyalty or is there something more to the sparring relationship between Kate and this charming man?

LIZ JONES—
CELEBRITY GOSSIP

Staff writer

In an unprecedented comeback, the Fortune family is back—and stronger than ever! Their mighty cosmetics empire has launched a new youth formula that women around the world are buying by the case, which firmly reestablishes Fortune Cosmetics as the number one international makeup company.

The Fortune family has also broken into the media business. They've purchased a television station as well as *this very* newspaper. There have been no staff changes except for one—Liz Jones has been relieved of her column. According to Kate Fortune, "There's no room in a serious paper for a rumor-spreading gossip monger."

This is the last week for the column to run. For those still interested in celebrity gossip, you may want to try *The Tattletale*. From now on, this section will be "Kate's Korner," featuring helpful tips on matchmaking, planning your wedding, raising your babies and home-decorating ideas.

We hope you enjoy the new direction of the column. Happy reading!

One

The entire view offended Rebecca Fortune. It was a dark and stormy night—how trite was that? Lightning speared the midnight sky, haloing a big, gaudy, ostentatious mansion that looked like a fake set in a grade B Hollywood movie. Worse yet, she was about to break into the mansion.

Rebecca wrote mysteries. She'd thrown her heroines into every dangerous situation her devious mind could come up with—and her imagination was considerable. But she'd throw her word processor in the trash before forcing a heroine into a stupid, clichéd plot setting like this.

Rain sluiced through her curly red hair, dribbled down her neck and splashed off her eyelashes. She was shivering all the way down to her squishy wet sneakers. March was usually chilly in Minnesota, but the whole day had been unseasonably warm, almost springlike. Before leaving home, she'd heard the storm forecast, but her raincoat was a neon yellow slicker—hardly suitable burglar attire—so she'd dressed for success in a black sweatshirt and black jeans. Both were clinging to her like soggy glue.

She must have been more miserable sometime.

She just couldn't remember when. Her extensive experience with crime—including a wide range of burglary techniques—had been acquired in her nice, safe, warm office, in front of a keyboard and all her research books. Reality was proving to be a teensy bit more difficult than theory.

She'd thought she'd planned this out so well.

The tall iron fence protecting the property was locked, but she'd just vaulted the fence. That was no sweat. Right after Monica Malone's murder, police and investigators had swarmed around the place. Now, though, there was little chance of anyone discovering her. The house was as closed up and quiet as a tomb, totally deserted—no sign anyone had lived or been around in weeks.

She'd brought a backpack full of helpful tools. The mansion had five outside entrances. Rebecca had tried a skeleton key on all the doors—she'd bought the key from one of her writers' catalogs—and that had been when things started going wrong. The key didn't work on any of the locks. She'd also brought a crowbar, because every resourceful heroine she'd ever written had found some use for a crowbar. Not her. She'd circled the whole blasted house, checking every window on the first floor. None of them were boarded up, but they were all locked tight. All she'd managed to do with the crowbar so far was chip some paint.

There were a dozen other tricks and tools in her backpack—her writing research had prepared her well for a life of crime. But as yet, none of them had been worth spit, and the pack weighed a ton, biting into her shoulder blades. The sky was a black growly mass of moving clouds, and thunder rumbled close enough to make the whole earth shudder—or maybe that was just her, shivering hard. Any sane woman, she told herself, would give up.

Unfortunately, Rebecca had always been rotten at giving up on anything that mattered to her. Some said she was stubborn to the point of being relentless. Rebecca preferred to think she took after her mother, Kate, who never failed to have the guts and character to do what she had to do.

This was something Rebecca *had* to do. There were certainly other people trying to clear her brother of the charge that he'd murdered Monica. But they weren't getting anywhere. No one outside the family really believed in Jake's innocence.

Her lips firmed with resolve, she tramped through the wet, spiky grass around the circumference of the house again. There had to be a way in. And, somehow, she had to find it.

A wild, gusty wind tore at her hair. When she lifted a hand to push the hair from her face, spears of lightning caught the sparkle of gold on her wrist. The charm bracelet belonged to her mother, not her, and a dozen turbulent, traumatic memories suddenly flashed in Rebecca's mind.

She'd almost lost her mom. The whole world had believed that Kate Fortune had died in a plane crash—no one had known she'd fought off a kidnapper and had survived the crash, only to be lost in the jungle for months—and Rebecca's heart still clenched tight when she remembered the tears, the fear, the *love* that had colored her recent emotional reunion with her mom. She'd taken the charm bracelet from the sculpted arm that had displayed it in the Fortune's office the day Kate was discovered missing.... She'd added her own charms once Kate's will had been read and each family member had received the charm that had represented his or her own birth. Rebecca had needed the connection the bracelet represented, and her mother hadn't let her give it back once she returned.

For Rebecca the charm bracelet was a talisman, a symbol of what family meant, and the links of love and loyalty that bound them all.

She rubbed those gold links now. Maybe her mother had founded a financial dynasty, but Kate loved children and believed in family before all else. She'd passed those unshakable values on to Rebecca. And right now was a heck of a time to be thinking about babies, but she was thirty-three, and babies pounced in her mind at any excuse these days. Her personal biological clock didn't seem to care that she was single, with no Prince Charming on the immediate horizon. She wanted a baby. She'd always wanted children and a family. No matter what exotic directions the rest of the Fortune clan had taken, she was a hopelessly nurturing homebody type. And now it seemed she was the last of the family to settle down. Even her nieces had kids!

Rocking a baby came naturally to her. Cat burglary sure didn't—and a sudden shiver of fear snaked up her spine. The storm didn't scare her. And she wasn't spooked by the big old deserted mansion, even if it was a murder site.

The shiver of fear was motivated solely by love. She wanted so badly to come through for her brother, and she was scared of failing. Somewhere in that house, there *had* to be clues, information, evidence—*something* that would clear Jake's name. Dozens of people had had outstanding reasons for killing the old bat, including quite a few in her own family. Monica had been an evil, greedy, selfish woman, and she'd done her damnedest to destroy the Fortune family for more than a generation. A two-year-old could have found suspects with motives.

The problem was that Monica had almost cost Jake everything that mattered to him, so he had a prize-winning motive, too. More to the point, he'd been at the scene of the murder and a ton of physical evidence pointed to him. Neither the cops nor the family's investigators had turned up another suspect. Neither had the staff of lawyers on her brother's team. No one seemed to regret that the aging Hollywood film star was dead, but neither did anyone believe in Jake's innocence.

In her heart, Rebecca knew her brother couldn't, wouldn't, kill anyone—no matter what the provocation. But she was afraid that unless she found proof that another suspect had done the deed, no one else would.

So far, she hadn't run across an alarm system, or any indication that one was turned on. The doors were all locked, and the first windows were not only latched and locked, but built casement-style, with small square panes made of leaded glass. Even if she broke the glass, the panes were too small for her to gain entry. With rain dribbling down her cheeks, she discounted the rose trellis—she was a lightweight 115 pounds, but the trellis looked beyond rickety. A huge silver maple spread a hoopskirt of branches in the yard, but no branches were close enough for her to leap to the east roof—unless she suddenly developed wings.

She could try the trellis if she had to. First, though, she circled the house again, crouching low, battling the bushes in the flower beds to shine a flashlight over one basement window at a time.

The prickers of a flowering almond snagged at her clothes like a witch's fingers, stabbing and clawing. Mud sucked at her sneakers. She broke a nail on a window frame. A splinter lodged in her finger, and the nuisance thing bled. The deluge finally quit, but she was so damp and cold that miserableness was only a matter of degree by that time, anyway.

Finally, though, her flashlight zoomed on a window frame that appeared both uneven and cracked. She battled a bosomy lilac bush for the space to crouch down, and ran her palm across the uneven frame. The window wasn't latched. It just seemed to be painted shut.

It opened out, and didn't look big enough for a ten-year-old to crawl through, but no matter. Rebecca figured this was as close to manna from heaven as she was likely to get.

She reached behind for her backpack, and juggled it and the flashlight to find her crowbar again. Twice she probed and pulled with the crowbar, but it was almost impossible to get leverage in the narrow space between the blasted wet lilac bushes. The muddy, mucky ground refused to help her out with some traction. On the third try, though, she finally managed to wedge the crowbar under the ledge, and the window squeaked and creaked open.

Rebecca hunkered back on her heels and scratched her chin. So. It was open. But the opportunity made her feel as if she were holding a winning lottery ticket without a way to collect the loot. The window opened out, creating an even tinier space to crawl through than she'd first guessed. She was built lean, but not *that* lean.

Hesitantly she aimed the flashlight through the opening. Spatial relationships weren't exactly her strength, but it sure looked like a hundred feet down to the concrete basement floor. Nothing to break her fall. Stephen King could have set a book down in those gloomy, eerie shadows. The light didn't illuminate anything but ghostly corners and dank concrete walls.

She was probably going to kill herself if she tried this.

On the other hand, this appeared to be her only way in—and backing down certainly wasn't an option. Her bones would just have to squish small enough to fit, and that was that.

She zipped the flashlight into the backpack, and dropped the pack inside.

It fell with a clattering thud. A long way down.

She swallowed a lump of fear thicker than tar, then moved. Shimmying on her back, trying to ignore the mud seeping into her sweatshirt, she poked her feet in first, then her legs, then wriggled her fanny in. Then came trouble. Her hips wedged in the opening, and suddenly she couldn't move. At all. In or out.

Cripes, there were times she'd groaned about not having enough hips to fill out a pair of jeans. Now she wished she'd had three less cherry doughnuts this week. Her fanny seemed stuck. No kidding, no joke, seriously stuck.

She briefly considered crying. Actually, she didn't *really* want to cry. She just wanted to be home. In a hot, soaking, sybaritic rose-scented bath, maybe with a glass of chablis, maybe reading some of the thick files of research information she'd picked up lately on sperm banks and fantasizing about babies.

Fantasizing about babies was tempting. Just not real helpful right then. Moving in either direction hurt, but lying still was just as untenable—her spine was screaming objections at being trapped in this contortionist position. It'd be nice if a hero would wander by to help, but that didn't seem real likely. Being crawled on by earthworms seemed far more likely...and that did it. The mental picture of the worms in that flower bed being close enough to crawl on her was mighty powerful incentive to move.

She sucked in a breath, swung her legs up, and pushed in hard.

The push worked. Sort of. She was still alive when she crash-landed on the concrete floor, but that measure of success was hardly worth applause. On the route down, she'd cracked her forehead on the window frame, and both her breasts had been squished and scraped. She landed on a hip and a wrist. The basement was darker than tar, with a dank, damp, mildewy smell. Wouldn't matter if she were in the Taj Mahal; she hurt too much to care. Stars danced in front of her eyes in a real dizzy tango. She wasn't positive it was possible to break a fanny—she'd certainly never seen one in a cast or in traction—but she was damned scared she'd done it.

To add insult to injury, a light suddenly flashed in her eyes.

The obnoxious glaring light came from a bald light bulb in the middle of the basement room.

And to top off the worst debacle she'd ever gotten herself into, the man standing by the light switch, shaking his head, was familiar. Painfully familiar. So was his unmistakably gravelly tenor.

"I thought at least ten kids were breaking into the place. You made enough noise to wake the dead. I should have known it was you. Dammit, Rebecca, what the *hell* are you doing here?"

Rebecca squeezed her eyes closed. "At the moment, I'm sitting here with forty-seven broken bones, feeling sorry for myself. Please, God, make this a nightmare, and when I wake up, try and fix it so he's someone else. Make him a Russian spy. Make him a serial killer. Make him anyone but Gabe Devereax."

Not that she was willing to open her eyes to check, but that dry, gravelley tenor seemed to be coming closer. "You're damn lucky it's me—and at least I have a logical reason for being here. Did you leave your brain at home? You could have killed yourself—or *gotten* yourself killed—and you look worse than an alley cat who's been in a street fight."

"Thank you for sharing that with me. I'm dying of pain and injuries, and all you can do is yell?"

"I'd yell a lot louder if I thought it'd do any good. For God's sakes, you're soaked and covered with mud and it looks like you're growing branches in your hair. If that isn't witless, I don't know what is. Quit fighting me, dammit. I'm just trying to see if you're hurt."

"I already *know* I'm hurt." But her pride was now smarting a dozen times more than any of her other scrapes and bruises. Gabe had stalked over and hunched down. Keeping her eyes closed and practicing denial had worked pretty well—until she felt his big strong hands feeling her up. Her eyes shot wide open then.

There were times and places when Rebecca wouldn't mind a guy feeling her up—at a fantasy level, she might even have entertained Gabe in that role—but not when she was being handled like a sexless sack of sugar. Merciless fingers probed and poked her ankles, trailed up her calf, bent her knee, lifted her arms, rotated her wrists.... She said "ouch" several times. Either he wasn't paying attention or he didn't believe her.

Possibly she'd have felt less resentful if he didn't look so good. Heaven knew how Gabe had gotten in the house, but she already knew he was resourceful. Spit. He was the best. That was why she'd convinced her family to have him look into her mother's disappearance. And although he hadn't come up with much in *that* case, he'd been more successful with some other family cases over the past few years. But now she had to look like something a dog would bury, and there wasn't a rip or a tear or a smudge of dirt on him. His clipped dark hair looked fresh-brushed, his square jaw fresh-shaved. His galloping shoulders stretched the seams of a long-sleeved navy T, but the shirt was tucked nearly into jeans. His boots didn't even look muddy.

Rebecca didn't know him well. She wasn't sure it

was possible for a woman to know a man's man like Gabriel Devereax well—but they'd crossed paths before. Several family members had already noted that they got along about as well as a snake and mongoose. Not only didn't Rebecca object to Gabe, she was the one who'd originally researched PI firms and urged her family to hire him. She knew, better than anyone, that Gabe had an unbeatable reputation and credentials. She respected him completely. But when her family had trouble, Rebecca was hardly going to take the back seat and let someone else drive.

Gabe appreciated advice about as much as poison ivy. What she called help, he called interference. Anyone with the most basic concept of family would understand that love and loyalty required her involvement. Trying to explain that to Gabe was like drilling a hole in granite. He had a handsome head, but there was a lot of stone between those ears.

Even if there was no love lost between them, Rebecca could hardly fail to notice certain details about that handsome head. He was thirty-eight, and he looked it. The square-boned jaw, the scar on his right temple, the brush strokes of character lines bracketing his eyes and mouth, all spoke of a man who'd lived hard. He was no boy. There was energy in that rugged face, vital, virile energy, and a never-backdown determination stamped in all those lonely lines on his brow.

Personally, Rebecca thought a woman would have to be an eensy bit bonkers to risk taking on any man as tough and closed up as Gabe Devereax...but the man did have the deepest, darkest, sexiest eyes she'd ever seen. At the moment, it was impossible to ignore those eyes, because they were aggravatingly, relentlessly focused on her face. He cupped her chin with a knuckle, and examined her face for injuries, with as much personal interest as he'd have shown a bug under a microscope.

"I think you're going to live," he announced. "Although it's pretty hard to tell for sure under all that dirt." Because he was looking straight in her eyes, she didn't instantly realize where his right hand was. Smoother than a card cheat's, his palm had sneaked under her sweatshirt. His hand was warm, volatilely, evocatively warm, and skimming an electric path over her ribs.

"*Hey.*" She moved faster than a 747 to push him away, but the ox wouldn't be pushed.

"Oh, don't get your liver in an uproar. If I were going to make a pass, you'd know it. Trust me, sex is only on my mind ninety percent of the time. You got a hell of a scrape here—and no, I'm not looking to see how far it goes up—but I want you to cough."

"Cough? I don't need to cough—"

"Well, we can just drive you to the emergency room and get those ribs x-rayed, but somehow, I didn't think you'd cotton to that idea. If it didn't hurt when you coughed, I might—might—be more reassured that rib isn't cracked, but hey, if you want to go get an X ray—"

She coughed. Exuberantly.

"You sure that didn't hurt?"

"Positive. And you can quit trying to threaten me, Gabe. It'd take you and the marines to get me anywhere near any stupid emergency room. I'm perfectly fine. I just had the wind knocked out of me."

"Yeah?" Gabe removed his hand, but he stayed hunched over her. "You've got a goose egg on your forehead, bloody scrapes all over the place, and you're so damned wet you're probably gonna catch pneumonia. The water's turned on upstairs, so we can at least clean up the cuts, but there's no telling if we'll find anything for you to dry off and warm up in. How bad's that forehead hurting? You dizzy? Seeing anything double?"

If the blasted man had any manners, he'd give her the chance to answer, but no. Obviously, Gabe wasn't going to take her word on anything, because he reached over and cupped her jaw so he could examine that goose-egg bump again. Fingertips feathered her hair back so that he could get a better look. Once he was finished playing doctor, his eyes met hers.

Rebecca wasn't sure what happened then. He couldn't have held her gaze for more than a few seconds, but the scowl disappeared from his brow. There was something in his expression. Something she'd never have expected. Something more than exasperation, something beyond Gabe Devereax's hopeless compulsion to take charge of anything in his path.

She was so wet and bedraggled that road kill would have to look more appealing. Yet there was something in those deep, dark eyes that punched the accelerator in her pulse.

If Gabe had even noticed she was a woman, he hadn't let on before. Suddenly she was having trouble breathing. Gabe was a vital, virile, potent masculine package—easy enough to enjoy sparring with, when there'd been absolutely no threat or thought of his noticing her in any personal way. She wasn't... easy around Gabe. Not as a woman. On the other hand, likely the fall had addled her brain. There couldn't have been a sillier time to feel a power surge of hormones, and common sense told her she was imagining that look in his eyes.

Still, her pulse engine was revving harder than a jalopy with no muffler when Gabe's expression abruptly changed. The scowl that popped back between his brows was even darker and more critical than the one before. He rocked back on his heels and then sprang to his feet. "Maybe you don't need a doctor. But let's see how you do when you try to stand up."

"Oh, for heaven's sake. I'm perfectly fine." She ignored his hand and promptly scrambled to a standing position. A bad mistake. The lump on her forehead instantly throbbed; her breasts and wrist smarted like fire, and now she knew for sure her fanny was broken. If threatened at knifepoint, though, she wouldn't have admitted feeling wobbly to Gabe. "How did *you* get in the house, anyway?"

"The way most people do. Legally." His tone was dry. "Eventually the estate's going on the market, but it's been closed up until all the probate tangles are over with. I called Monica Malone's lawyer. Gave him my credentials, told him I believed there had to be more evidence in the house connected to the lady's murder, and asked if he'd mind if I looked around personally. He gave me the key."

"That's it? That's all you had to do to get a key?" It seemed so unfair.

"Now, Rebecca, everyone can't be gifted with a writer's imagination and fondness for high drama. Some of us even tend to do things the simple, normal, boring way—you know, by using basic common sense and logic?"

"Amazing. I could swear we had this exact same conversation before."

"Yeah, we did. It didn't get through to you then, either." He shifted past her to close the gaping basement window. "We'll get you cleaned up, and then you're going home."

"Only in your dreams, cutie. I didn't just risk life and limb to disappear on your orders." She was pretty sure no one had ever dared to call Gabe Devereax "cutie" before. The epithet seemed to startle, then amuse, him. For all that he was a hopelessly overbearing macho type—and probably untrainable, from a woman's standpoint—he'd always had a redeeming sense of humor.

"Speaking of orders—as I'm sure you know—I'm here on your family's. As outlandish and outrageous as it sounds, they actually trust me to follow through with this investigation all by myself. Can you imagine? Just because it's my job and I've got over ten years of experience and professional qualifications behind me?"

Rebecca reached down for her backpack of tools. God, he was sassy. She might have been tempted to laugh—if the subject wasn't so serious. "I trust you, too, Sherlock," she said honestly. "You're wonderful at what you do. But it isn't your brother who's been charged with murder. It's mine. And I love him. And until his name is cleared, I can't just sit home and knit booties. Did you find anything in the house so far?"

"I haven't had the chance to look around. I'd just turned the key when I heard all hell breaking loose down here. Now, of course, I don't know why I didn't immediately guess it was you." His face was in shadow when he scrubbed a tired hand over it. "Rebecca, listen to me."

"I'm listening." But she admitted it warily.

"This isn't the first time I've been here. I assume you know I've been on the job from the day your brother was charged. I was here during the cops' investigation, and after, when the yellow tape went down, I combed this place from stem to stern. This is my third run-through. So far, every shred of evidence points to Jake being guilty."

"I know." The knowledge was like a needle in her chest.

"Love and objectivity don't mix. I know you want to help your brother. But I'm not putting you down when I say you'd be better off at home, knitting those booties. You could get hurt, messing around with this."

Her gaze scanning the shadows, Rebecca vaguely noted a behemoth of a furnace, pipes, dampness seeping into the foundation walls—and the bottom edge of some wooden stairs, leading up. She heard Gabe, but what she heard in his voice only magnified her resolve. He would do his job. She'd never doubted that. But he didn't believe in Jake's innocence, any more than the police did.

She paused a second before aiming for the stairs, and pushed a fistful of tangled curls off her face. "You're right about my not being objective. I have no interest whatsoever in being objective. If you'll remember, Gabe, I'm the one who first tracked down your PI agency for the family, when my mother was in that plane crash."

"I remember."

She nodded. "No one believed that Kate was alive. No one believed she could be. And I wanted you hired, because you're the best, and I always respected that you could do certain things that I can't. But when you took on that job, you didn't believe

me about my mother being alive. You were no different than everyone else. Who was right that time,
Devereax?''

"You were. But that was completely different—''

She shook her head, swiftly and violently, making
the lump on her forehead ache like a bear—but she
didn't care. "It's exactly the same thing. You trust
your head, the same way I trust my heart. It's because I love my brother that I know positively he
never murdered anyone…and I don't care how rotten
Monica Malone was, or what she did to him.''

Gabe sighed. One of those exasperating masculine
sighs that expressed centuries of archaic attitudes
about women—and particularly her. "There are a
few minor flaws in that logic, but we'll forget those
and move along. If you believe your brother's innocent—and that all the physical evidence against
him is just an inconvenient fantasy—that would
mean that the real murderer is running around loose.
A damn good reason to stay out of this. You could
be in danger if you start poking your nose in fires
you're not qualified or prepared to put out.''

"For cripes' sake, Gabe. That's why I'm here. To
find those fires.''

"God, it's like talking to a marshmallow. Nothing
gets through.'' For the second time, he washed his
face with an exhausted hand. "Somehow I have the
feeling I'm not going to be able to talk you into
going home.''

"Now, now." She patted his shoulder consolingly—as she hiked past him toward the basement stairs. "I'm going to help you. Trust me."

TWO

Rebecca was as much help as a tornado. Given an option between the two evils, Gabe would have chosen the less chaotic.

That wasn't the redhead.

For the second time, he dipped the washcloth under the faucet, wrung it out and aimed the cool cloth at the lump on her forehead. Rain was still battering the windows like bullets. March was early for a thunderstorm in Minnesota. No point in complaining; at least it was rain, instead of snow. Still, thunder shuddered through the house, and the lights winked and blinked at every flash of lightning. They'd be lucky if they didn't lose the electricity altogether.

Losing the electricity wouldn't bother him. Gabe was a resourceful man. He'd spent years in the Special Forces proving his ability to cope in even the most impossible of situations. Danger had never stopped him. Neither had adversity. He'd never counted on luck or God to solve a problem—in the past.

Conceivably, though, a few concentrated hours with Rebecca Fortune could turn even a hard-core heathen into a praying man.

"Yee-ouch. What, did you take lessons under Torquemada? Leave me alone, you bully."

He didn't stop working, didn't look up. Right now, Rebecca was propped up on the kitchen counter, her face tilted toward the sink light.

He had a clear view of the gash on her forehead, but the chances of keeping her pinned and still for long wouldn't make bookie odds. "It's your own damn fault it hurts. There's little specks of something in the cut. Maybe paint from that window frame. They have to come out. If you'd quit squirming, I'd get done a lot faster. I think you need a couple of stitches—"

Her response was swift. "No."

"And since God knows what you connected with to get all those scrapes, you probably need a tetanus shot—"

Her response was even swifter. "I had one a couple of weeks ago."

"Sure you did. And cats swim. You've got a real talent for fiction—which is a good thing, since I don't think you're gonna make it as a career criminal. Breaking and entering doesn't seem to be your thing at all."

"Don't you start again with me, Devereax. I did this for my brother, and it wouldn't matter to me if I'd ended up with all four limbs in casts and traction—I'd do it again."

Gabe believed her. That was what scared him.

Most people could be appealed to through reason.

Most women had a concept of safety, personal limitations, how to protect themselves. Bring that stuff up with Rebecca and she went blank. Nobody home in those pretty green eyes. No synapse connections indicating any brain function at all.

He dropped the washcloth and angled her face toward the sink light to study the welt again. Finally, it looked clean, but the ugly gash marring that soft, cream white skin made him furious. At her.

The punch-in-the-gut response to touching that soft, cream white skin made him even more furious. At himself.

When a man was standing between a woman's thighs, an arousal was a natural, unavoidable biological reaction. Gabe understood perfectly well why he was harder than a hammer. And one day out of 365, a guy was entitled to feel unreasonable for a couple of minutes.

But he was mad at her for that, too.

When he stepped back, Rebecca mistakenly seemed to assume she was free and promptly leaned forward. "If you get off that counter, you die," he informed her. "You need a bandage on that."

"Sheesh. It's just a little lump. It can't be worth all this trouble."

"If it isn't taped right, you'll get a scar."

"My brother's in jail on a murder one charge. Who the patooties could care about a stupid little scar? We've wasted enough time on this thing."

"One more minute and this'll be done." He

stepped between her thighs again. He had to. He didn't trust Rebecca not to fly off the counter and start playing sleuth. He'd found the makings of a butterfly bandage in the antiquated first aid box. Leaning this close to her, Geronimo naturally stood at attention again, as stiff as a warrior's lance.

Like his namesake, Geronimo should have figured out by now that a guy couldn't win every time. Gabe ignored that problem. He wished he could ignore her.

She was relatively cleaned up now. Technically, no one was supposed to remove anything from the estate until all the legal tangles surrounding Monica Malone's death were settled. Those legal complications meant that the cupboards and drawers and closets in the house were still jammed with stuff. Gabe had had no trouble finding a towel, washcloth, the first aid supplies and some clothes. He'd also caught sight of some thirty-year-old Scotch in the top kitchen cupboard.

He was considering leveling it.

"You done?" she said hopefully.

"Yeah, I'm done."

"Gabe...thanks. I really couldn't see the cut myself, not at the angle it was. I didn't mean to be a pistol. I appreciate the help."

"No sweat." A total lie, Gabe thought. Everything about her was a sweat.

Rebecca wasn't vain or spoiled, he gave her that—and she sure as hell could have been both, given the enormous wealth and affluence of the Fortune family.

It wasn't her fault that she'd never been outside a protected environment. Her background just made her inescapable trouble. She was a hopeless idealist, plenty bright, but no street smarts, no practical life experience. She'd never run across the seamier, more realistic side of life. She'd never been near it. She was a believer in love, in white knights and honor, and as far as Gabe could tell, she didn't have a clue that there were predators out there who could hurt her.

Worse yet, she fancied herself a Nancy Drew, just because she'd written a few mystery novels. The complications she could cause, "helping" with this investigation regarding her brother, were enough to give Gabe an ulcer.

So was she.

As she slid off the counter, his eyes homed on the view of a lace-trimmed bra and the shadow of cleavage. More shadow than cleavage. There'd been no way he could talk her into peeling off the muddy, soaking-wet sweatshirt until he found something else for her to put on—he'd yanked the V-necked black sweater from a drawer upstairs, and he assumed it had belonged to Monica Malone. The late Monica, like so many of the Hollywood glamour stars of her era, had been built like a battleship on the upstairs deck.

The V neck gaped on Rebecca as if she were an orphan waif playing dress-up. Her black jeans were finally dry, and snug enough to outline long, lean legs and a nonexistent tush. Since she couldn't sit without squirming, he strongly suspected she'd bruised that bitsy tush, but for damn sure she'd never admit it to him. There was far more pride than sense in those soft green eyes, and that about summed up the rest of her appearance, too.

The face was valentine-shaped, the skin too white, the eyes too dark, a mouth that looked dangerously butter-soft, and a nose with an impertinent tip. He guessed her height at around five-five. A respectable height—except next to him—but it was hard to resist calling her "shorty" when the least teasing got such a rise out of her.

Her hair was dark cinnamon, and at the moment layered to her shoulders in a snarled tangle of curls. She'd obviously had no chance or time to brush it, but he'd spent time with her before this, and he knew her hair always looked like she'd just climbed out of a man's bed after a long, acrobatic night. Since she was a Fortune, there was no question that she had the money for a decent haircut, so apparently she just didn't think about it. Maybe a haircut wouldn't help. Give her a butch cut and drape her in iron—she was still going to look skinny, sexy, half put together and, dammit, vulnerable.

Gabe had never been attracted to vulnerable-looking females, so he had no idea why she so revved his engines—and he didn't want to know. If and when a man was inclined to make a mistake, Gabe generally theorized, he might as well get his money's worth and do it right. But, hell, not with her. He'd tangled with his share of women, and at thirty-eight he certainly knew when a risk was worth taking. He liked risk and he wasn't short on guts— but no way was he a suicidal kamikaze pilot.

"Rebecca..." He swiped a hand over his face again. As fast as she'd sprung down from the counter—as he should have known—she was galloping toward the door. "Where are you going?"

"Anywhere. Everywhere. I thought I'd check out the scene of the murder first—it was in the living room, wasn't it? Then see what I could pry and poke up in Ms. Malone's bedroom."

"If you're headed for the living room, better aim right instead of left. Unless you have some interest in the pantry and butler's quarters. And listen, Nancy D. You leave stuff as you find it. You don't take anything. I'd rather you didn't even touch anything without telling me—"

"Sheesh, Gabe. I've read a dozen books on police procedure. If I find anything remotely related to evidence, I sure as Pete know enough not to mess it up."

"Somehow your reading those books doesn't reassure me too much."

For a vulnerable woman, she had the unholiest grin. "I know, cutie. You really can't seem to help being a take-charge, overbearing, overprotective pain. Especially with women. God, thinking about you being a father just boggles the mind. You'd drive a daughter nuts, sweetie pie.''

"Since I don't plan to be a father, the problem is moot. Babies are the last thing on my mind.''

"Yet another core difference between us—no surprise. If it weren't for this immediate problem with my brother, babies'd be front-line priority for me. You should see all the research material I've been collecting on sperm banks.''

"Sperm banks? You can't be serious.''

"On the subject of babies, I couldn't be more serious.'' But she grinned again. "However, the only reason I mentioned sperm banks was because I couldn't resist—I just *knew* you'd get that look on your face, darlin'. But right now, time's wasting...and babies just have no place on this night's agenda.''

No, Gabe thought darkly, murder was apparently front-line on the lady's agenda now. And only Rebecca could bounce from sperm banks to murder in a single breath.

Well, he wasn't going to follow her around. He had an investigative job he was being paid to do, and his salary didn't extend to baby-sitting imaginative, recalcitrant redheads—even if she was kin to his boss.

He headed for the office—and yeah, he knew the mansion had one, because he'd been here before. The wallpaper was textured silk, the windows were hung with poofy, powder-puff-looking curtains, and the desk had a brocade chair. It was about the sissiest office he'd ever been in, and he doubted Monica Malone had ever paid a bill on her own, least of all in here. Either the cops or the lawyers had absconded with every record or financial statement in the file cabinets, as Gabe already knew. Still, he flicked on the fancy offset lighting and started yanking out drawers.

Someone could have missed something. Someone always did. As much evidence as had emerged in the case, there were still huge holes and gaps in information. He carefully, meticulously tore the place apart...for about twenty minutes.

About then he realized how silent it was in the rest of the house. Dead silent. Ideal for concentrating, except that it nagged at him like a bee sting that he couldn't hear Rebecca. Her labeling him overbearing still rankled. He wasn't *remotely* overbearing. He simply had ample previous experience with Rebecca—enough to know she was impulsively, unwittingly capable of causing no end of trouble. When a man was in the same house with a nuclear reactor, he was perfectly justified in worrying.

He found her in the long, sweeping living room, huddled in a chair, staring at the marble fireplace. Damn woman. She looked up at him with huge dark eyes. "I'm just trying to picture it. I know she was killed here...."

"Yes."

"We know Jake was here. And that he was drunk.

We know they argued, physically argued. Jake said Monica scratched him and came at him with a letter opener, and he had a stab wound in the shoulder to prove it. He admitted that he pushed her, that she fell against that marble fireplace and hit her head.''

"Monica and your brother's fingerprints were all over the scene.'' Gabe didn't add that no one else's identifiable fingerprints had surfaced. Rebecca already seemed to have a pretty good picture of the compelling evidence against her brother. She couldn't seem to stop wringing those slim white hands.

"But he said Monica was alive when he left her. Natalie, his daughter, saw him later. We talked to him. It wasn't like a fight, not on his part. He only pushed her because she was attacking him with that letter opener, and he had no *reason* to lie about her still being alive. He could have claimed self-defense if she'd died accidentally in a struggle like that. I'm telling you, someone else was either already in the house or came in after Jake left. My brother did *not* kill her, Gabe.''

Gabe crossed the room to the art deco bar. Nothing back there was quite as good as the thirty-year-old Scotch he'd found in the kitchen, but at the moment he'd have settled for Kentucky moonshine. Not for him. Being around Rebecca predictably inspired him to drink, but the immediate problem was the damn heartsick look in her eyes.

He splashed some whiskey in a cut-crystal shot glass and carried it over to her.

She took the glass and sniffed it. "Yuck," she said.

"Shut up and level it, shorty."

"If you call me 'shorty' one more time..." she began, but then her voice trailed off. It was truly a landmark occasion—she actually didn't bristle up and argue with him. Instead, she lifted the shot glass and chugged the brew in an impressive three gulps. Once she finished coughing, she wiped her eyes with a shudder. "Personally, I'm with Mary Poppins. If you have to take medicine, you should be able to add a spoonful of sugar to it."

Imagining the taste of whiskey and sugar was enough to make *him* shudder, but he could see that the liquid courage did its job. Color shot back into her cheeks. She quit trying to knit those hands into a sweater. Gabe figured if there was ever going to be a two-second window when she could handle a dose of realism, it had to be now. "No other suspects have surfaced, Rebecca—not a single name, much less a clear fingerprint. All the physical evidence points to Jake...and he had motive."

"Monica was blackmailing him. I know. Milking him for shares of the Fortune company, from the time she found out Jake was born on the wrong side of the blanket. If she exposed him, he was afraid he'd lose everything. I know all the family dirty linen, Gabe, and I know the mistakes my brother made. I know he'd been drinking a lot and had been screwing up at work. That the pressure split up his marriage, and set him against Nate. It still doesn't mean he killed her."

It was pretty rare that two and two didn't add up to four, Gabe thought, but it was hard to argue with such blind loyalty. "I just thought you might need to recognize how bad it looks," he said gently.

She surged out of the chair, suddenly as restless as a wet cat. "You know what I recognize? That Monica Malone has somehow managed to hurt my family for two generations—she's dead now, and it still isn't over. The old witch was guilty of kidnapping, sabotage, infidelity, stalking, theft, blackmail—you name it, she did it against the Fortune family, starting way back when she had an affair with my father. I swear she's hurt us for the last time. It's got to stop."

"Rebecca," he said patiently, "go home."

"No."

"Maybe you're right. Maybe someone did come in this house after your brother left, and murdered her. But if there's a shred of proof in this house pointing in that direction, I promise I'll find it."

"I know you would try. And I know you're good. But you don't have a woman's eye, Gabe. There's every chance I could see things that you couldn't."

He scrubbed a hand over his face. No point in continuing in *that* direction, so he tried another. "There's a tiny element you may not have considered, Red. Finding evidence that someone else murdered Monica doesn't mean you're going to be any happier. I know the whole story of how she preyed on your family. But that's the point. If there *is* another suspect, it could well be another member of your clan. There's no shortage of motives all through the Fortune family."

"It wasn't any of us," Rebecca said firmly.

"I hate to tell you this, but it'd be tough to prove that viewpoint in court. Some misguided folk might think you were coming from blind loyalty instead of from rational, objective thinking."

"Well, they'd be wrong. That woman was a greedy, selfish, conniving shrew her whole life, Gabe. She could have had a thousand enemies besides us. And...oh God, I can't just sit here.... I'm going to start looking."

She shot toward the door and out before he could stop her. Not that Gabe would have tried. Reasoning with the woman was like trying to get through to a mule. He cast a longing glance at the bottle of whiskey.

He didn't believe she would find any evidence clearing her brother, but there was a slim chance it existed. And if the thousand-to-one odds that Rebecca was right paid off, there was still a real murderer out there. A cold-blooded killer wouldn't likely appreciate anyone poking and probing for the truth. Gabe had never mentioned that threat of danger to

Rebecca, but the nasty, rotten thought crossed his mind that *someone* had better watch over her.

It wasn't his problem. If worse came to worst, he could sic her mama on her. Kate Fortune could make a battalion of marines behave with a look.

It was just for this night that he was stuck with her. When he got home, there'd be ample time to dip into a consoling shot of whiskey. While he *had* to be around Rebecca, he definitely needed all the wits he could beg, borrow or steal.

Rebecca propped her fists on her hips. Monica Malone's bedroom was about what she'd expected—a study in a vain, greedy, self-indulgent woman.

Monica's world had definitely revolved around Monica. She had two oil portraits of herself on the wall, for Pete's sake. Walk-in closets stuffed with plunging necklines and more shoes than Madame Marcos. The bed was heart-shaped—how corny could you get?—with satin sheets and a plump satin headboard. Probably had to kill a whole whale to get all the bones and wiring in her corsets; the aging Monica had definitely been into pushing up, shoving out and, above all else, displaying her boobs. The vanity was sardine-packed with more bottles and vials than a cosmetic company could produce—and since the Fortune family had founded a dynasty in cosmetics, Rebecca ought to know.

She'd already rifled the drawers and closets. While she was in the sybaritic malachite bathroom, she'd also yanked down her jeans—away from Gabe's eagle eyes—to figure out why her fanny was hurting so much. There were certainly enough mirrors to display a nasty bruise already turning rainbow colors. Her forehead throbbed, her behind was killing her, and the long scrape on her chest and ribs refused to stop smarting.

Well, she could soak once she got home. Now wasn't the time. She refused to admit to being exhausted, even though it had to be three in the morning. Thunder boomed outside. The frustrated scowl on her forehead was just as dark and gloomy as the pitchy, witchy night outside.

Gabe didn't believe there was any evidence to find, she knew. He didn't want her around. She knew that, too. The rancid slug of whiskey had finally warmed her from the inside, though, renewing her determination. For some idiotic reason, she'd actually hoped Gabe might believe in her brother's innocence. It was obvious he didn't—no different from everyone else.

It wasn't the first time Rebecca had felt alone. As her gaze scanned the width of the room, she automatically rubbed the gold charm bracelet on her wrist. The symbol of family always sustained her. As diverse as the Fortune clan was, Rebecca had always felt different, not one to fit in or follow anyone else's pattern or values. It didn't matter. It had never mattered. Family meant loyalty. Love. The precious and unbreakable bonds of blood. She'd find a way to clear her brother's name or die trying. There'd never been any question about it.

Looking around, she rubbed and rerubbed the gold chain, idly wondering if Gabe even had a family. He never spoke of siblings or family members. Neither a wife nor babies seemed anywhere on his priority list. He came across as a self-sufficient loner, but in some quiet corner of her mind, Rebecca sensed that he was a deeply lonely man.

He'd undoubtedly crack up if she dared suggest such a thing, she thought, and then, abruptly, she forgot Gabe. Her eyes shot to her bracelet, then swiftly around the room. Jewelry. That woman had to have a ton of it. Undoubtedly the expensive stuff was stored in safe-deposit boxes—or the lawyers had absconded with it through the whole estate probate thing. But Monica had never been photographed when she wasn't decked out in trinkets and baubles of all kinds. Surely there had to be some jewelry boxes around here.

There were.

She found two freestanding jewelry chests in the back of one closet—both packed to the gills. Crouching down, she pulled out all the little drawers and started pawing through yards of glittery bangles and cheap baubles.

Her mood picked up anticipation. No, she didn't know what she was looking for, didn't know where to look, didn't even know if there was anything to find. But if there were secrets to find about Monica,

Rebecca strongly intuited they were in this bedroom. Maybe a guy hid secrets in his truck or his desk, but a woman always stored her secrets in her bedroom. It was her cache, her stash, her private hideaway, in a way a man would never understand.

In the fourth drawer down, her fingertips hit a bump. She ran over it again. Definitely a bump. Hustling, she upturned the drawer of baubles on the white closet carpet, shook the drawer good and then peered into the bottom. The bump showed up as a ripple in the satin lining.

The satin lining ripped out as easily as a candy wrapper.

Several snips of paper drifted out with it. One was a telegram so old that the yellow paper looked like a wrinkled napkin—some poor misguided dude announcing he loved Monica. Rebecca tossed that, then reached for the next—a love letter from another guy, who'd signed himself "Your faithful hound." She wondered dryly if the guy had been a dog as a lover, but then studied it more seriously. The love note was dated ten years before, too old to be of any relevance that she could imagine, but she tucked it near her knee anyway. If Monica valued the thing enough to hide it, it might mean something.

Most of the paper scraps were simply personal memorabilia, nothing that Rebecca could imagine having even a remote relationship to the woman's murder. Rebecca grimaced as she found more evidence of Monica's perfidy. She found proof that

Monica had been behind the attempted theft of the secret youth formula, had encouraged Allie's stalker, had people break in the lab and had even been behind the threats to deport Fortune scientist Nick Valkov— a threat that had prompted their marriage, the first of the rash of weddings in the Fortune family. At least Monica had done *something* right. But none of this was any use in clearing Jake's name.

Until she came to the letter. Adrenaline pumped through her veins as she read, then reread, the last missive.

It was a carbon copy of a letter, written not to Monica, but by Monica. Although the message contained only a few short lines, it was dated ten days before her death, threatening a woman named Tammy Diller about ''showing up for their meeting'' or risking ''more trouble than you ever dreamed of.''

Pay dirt.

Elation thrummed through Rebecca's pulse. Something about the woman's name struck a vague chord in her memory, but she couldn't place it...and that didn't immediately matter, anyway. The letter itself was enough. Maybe the missive was no proof that her brother was innocent. Maybe it wasn't proof this Tammy woman had done anything, either. But it was sure proof that another person had been in the picture around the time of Monica's death...and their relationship hardly sounded amicable.

Ignoring every ache and pain, Rebecca scrambled to her feet. Handling the letter as if it were precious china, she jogged out of the bedroom and into the hall, yelling loudly for Gabe.

Later it occurred to her that her screaming might have aroused his alarm and made him think she'd done something to half kill herself, because she saw him fly up the winding front stairs three at a time. Just then, the only things on her mind were elation and relief and excitement that she'd found something real and concrete that could link someone else to Monica's murder besides her brother.

When Gabe flew toward her, she flew straight at him.

It was perfectly logical to throw her arms around him. Any woman would have understood the perfectly natural, emotional impulse.

Gabe, though, didn't quite seem to see it that way.

Three

The way Rebecca was charging down that hall, Gabe naturally assumed demons or monsters were after her—or a killer. Maybe he'd been retired from the Special Forces for the past seven years, but certain responses were as well-honed as instincts for him. He was braced to yank her behind him, out of harm's way, and protect her. He was braced to confront serious danger.

He was braced for just about anything but the damn fool woman throwing her arms around him. The exuberant hug was so sudden. And maybe she aimed that sassy smack for his cheek, but it collided an inch short. On his mouth. With the impact of a bullet.

Gabe had been shot. Twice. The experience was something a man never forgot, although it hadn't hurt either time—not at the instant of impact. It had felt more like a sudden burn, a burst of stunning heat.

Bullets had nothing on Rebecca.

He'd known she was trouble. Known at some gut-instinct level that keeping his hands off her could avert the core source of that trouble. But initially he grabbed her because his brain was responding to the threat of danger. Initially adrenaline was pumping through his veins at the speed of light. A millisecond later, that adrenaline rush was sabotaged by the flooding pump of straight testosterone.

The long hall was dim and dark, so empty that his heartbeat echoed loudly, bouncing off the silence. Whyever in hell she'd hugged him, her head suddenly reared back. Velvet green eyes connected with his. The huge smile curving her lips suddenly faded, softened. She didn't drop her arms. She didn't do anything any sane, normal, rational woman would do. She lifted up on tiptoe, not unlike a kitten hellbent on being curious, and kissed him.

She tasted like spring winds and innocence. She tasted like nothing that had been in Gabe's life for a long, long time...nothing he'd missed or even wanted, dammit. Until that moment. Her mouth was softer than a baby's behind, the scent of her skin as wholesome as Ivory soap, and something was in one of the hands that scratched his neck. Paper? But her other hand suddenly clutched the dark hair at his nape, and her small breasts flattened against his chest, and suddenly Gabe couldn't breathe.

All right, he tried telling himself. It's all right. There was nothing happening here but a little overflow of testosterone. Just hormones. He'd been celibate for a while, and he damn well hated being celibate, and even if Rebecca drove him nuts, she was two-hundred-percent female. The sizzle of desire bolting through his system was natural. Simple biology.

Nothing seemed real simple at that moment, though. His fingers found their way into that messy tangle of red hair, so silky, so soft, and her mouth opened under the pressure of his. Her tongue was wet, as small as a secret, and if that woman had a repressive instinct in her, it didn't show. She kissed with abandon. She kissed like pure, untouched emotion. She kissed like she'd never been on a rollercoaster ride before and was utterly captivated by the whole experience.

Rebecca could totally immerse a man in quicksand in three seconds flat—if he let her.

Gabe twisted his mouth free, and sucked in a lungful of oxygen. Then tried sucking in another lungful. Then tried a more intelligent move—like removing his hands from her body and swearing.

Swearing worked. She opened her eyes, staring at him as if her vision were submerged in a fog, but her hands slowly dropped from his shoulders. It seemed a year or two later before she got around to rocking back on her heels. "Well," she murmured.

He didn't like the way she said that "Well." He didn't trust the way her right eyebrow suddenly arched, either.

"If I'd known you kissed like that, cutie pie, I'd have pressed for a sample long before this," she announced.

God give him strength. "It was an accident."

"I know."

"It won't happen again."

"The wonder was that it happened at all. Every time I've been around you before, I was pretty sure you were more tempted to kill me than kiss me."

"I was. I am. And if you hadn't been living a sheltered life hunched over a keyboard, you'd have known the chemistry was there. Where I come from, you don't wake up a sleeping lion. Now I assume, five miles back, you must have had some reason for throwing your arms around me?"

"Reason?" She said the word like it was alien. With Rebecca, that was certainly possible. For one long, horrifying minute, her soft green eyes stayed glued to his face, studying him, making him feel aggravatingly...naked. But then she blinked, and abruptly lifted her hand, as if just then remembering she was holding a piece of paper. "Of course I had a reason. A superb reason. Gabe! You won't believe what I found!"

Well, she was diverted from talking about all that touchy, tricky chemistry business, but calming Rebecca down when she was excited had a lot in common with containing a rumor in Washington.

Gabe saw the letter, read the letter, was dragged into Monica's bedroom closet, where she'd found the letter, but even after they headed back downstairs, she was prancing with energy—and trying hard to make him eat crow.

"Did I tell you I'd find something? Did I?"

"Now listen, shorty, you're getting your hopes sky-high. This really isn't proof of anything—"

"It's proof that there could have been another factor involved in Monica's murder. It's proof that someone besides my brother was butting heads with Monica in the same general time period around her death."

Yeah, he saw it that way, too. And it burned his butt that an idealistic, altruistic hopeless dreamer of a mystery writer had managed to find the clue instead of him—especially since he'd turned the damn mansion upside down himself three times now, and come up with *nada.*

Because Gabe wasn't born yesterday, he carefully sneaked the letter away from her and folded it neatly in his pocket. A Los Angeles address for this Tammy Diller had been on it, an address Rebecca had certainly seen—but hopefully wouldn't remember. The back of his mind was already clicking with plans. As soon as he got home, he could probe the data bases on the computer for info on that name and address. If anything panned out, he'd need to make travel arrangements for a trip to L.A.

First, though, he had to get rid of Rebecca. How a woman could still be so fired up in the middle of the night was beyond him—especially a woman who looked like she'd tangled with a whole gang in a back alley. Her face was as white as a virgin's wedding dress, and the gash on her forehead was clearly swelling under the bandage.

"You never believed I'd find anything, now did you? Just like you didn't believe me about my mother months ago. Logic isn't *always* more valuable than intuition, love bug. A woman and a man simply think differently. Even if I hadn't read a ton of reference books on crime-solving, sometimes a woman can just sense things—"

When she had to stop to take a breath, he broke in." I admit it. You did good. But it's going on 4:00 a.m. I think it's time we called this a night."

"You mean go home?" From the look on her face, the idea was as appealing as a case of chicken pox.

"I'm beat. I'm ready to pack this in, and I'm sure not leaving you alone here. You got a good lead—" he hastened to get that in, before she could praise herself for another hour and a half on the subject "—and as soon as I catch a few hours' rest, I'll run with it."

"Well, I agree, if you're beat, you should go home. But I could stay and keep looking a little longer. Maybe Monica had some other hiding places—"

"Maybe she did. But that's a needle-in-a-haystack possibility, considering all the people who've been over this place. And the letter is something concrete that can be pursued immediately. Besides which, we've been at this for hours—"

"I'm not tired," she immediately assured him. He saw the mutinous thrust of her chin.

His chin was bigger, and his scowl had a long

history of intimidating potential mutineers before.
"The hell you aren't. You look like the battered loser
in a cat fight, and you're not going to tell me that
you aren't starting to feel those bruises. That bump
on your forehead alone has to hurt like a bitch. Now
where's your car?"

She didn't look even nominally intimidated, but
the question effectively distracted her. "About a mile
past the main gate. There was a bunch of big old
walnut trees that made for a perfect dark place to
park. And if I parked that far away, I figured no one
would see me when I climbed the fence—"

"I don't want to hear any more about your break-
ing-and-entering debacle." God, she was going to
give him gray hair. Until meeting her, he'd considered himself a relatively young thirty-eight. There'd
been nothing to turn his hair white but death, destruc-
tion, and a few terrorists from his Special Forces
days. "Wherever your car is, it sounds too far to
walk. Mine's parked out front, so I'll just drive you
there. Now where'd you leave your wet sweatshirt?"

"In the kitchen." She glanced down at the black
V-neck sweater, and abruptly clutched the neck
closed. Heaven knew why. He'd seen her bra, seen
her cleavage, seen every inch of her long white throat
more than once tonight. Geronimo persisted in responding to her, no matter what repression techniques Gabe tried.

"I'd better put my sweatshirt back on, but where
should I put the sweater back?"

"Just keep the sweater. I can't imagine anyone would know or care if you borrowed it. I'll get it from you and return it sometime, but putting on a wet sweatshirt on a cold night doesn't make any sense. Just grab it—and that packsack you carried in with you—so we can go."

"I think I may have left a light on upstairs. And I have some stuff to clean up in the closet. And I'd better wash out that shot glass—"

There was a reason Gabe always worked alone. His employees were good at teamwork, and often enough his staff paired up for different projects. Not him. He just didn't like depending on other people. He liked being able to move fast and streamlined.

By the time Rebecca was "done" with all her messing around, he could have finished a slowpoke sucker.

He ushered her outside, turned to lock up the front door, and motioned her toward the long, low antique Morgan.

She wolf-whistled. Almost as good as a man. "*What* a darling," she murmured.

"Yeah, she is. '55. But she was cosseted as a showpiece for most of those years, so she doesn't have that many miles on her."

"You can still get parts?"

"Not easily. Parts are not only hard to find, they cost an arm and a leg. Damn few antique dealers even know this breed of car anymore."

"But you don't care, do you? She's worth all the trouble."

"Yeah." He hadn't expected Rebecca to understand. He opened the passenger door and watched her long, slim legs disappear under the long, slim console. The aggravating thought crossed his mind that she was made for the car.

Lack of sleep was obviously the reason he wasn't thinking clearly. He closed her in, locked her door and hiked around to the other side. The engine purred as soon as he turned the key.

"What a beautiful baby," she murmured.

Her comment about babies inevitably reminded him of the comment she'd made earlier about sperm banks. He told himself to keep quiet, that it was none of his business...but the comment had nagged at the back of his mind all night.

For a few minutes, he stayed silent. The storm had died, but a fine silver mist was still drizzling down. Grass and trees glistened in the ghostly night as he tooled down the driveway, stopping to unlock the gate with a set of keys. No one seemed to be awake or alive for miles. There were no lights, and no sounds but the rustling trees and the whisper of that diamond-studded mist.

Locating her car was easy; there were no other vehicles on the road. He pulled up behind the cherry red Ciera and glanced at her. She'd raved pretty enthusiastically about his car, and coming from the Fortune family, she could probably have owned a fleet of Morgans if she chose. Instead, she'd picked solid, reliable wheels. A wholesome four-door, yet. A capital *F* family car—for a lady who made no secret of her desire and love for family—and somehow he just couldn't let it go.

"You *aren't* serious about looking into sperm banks."

"Sure I am." While the engine idled, she ducked her head to gather up her things.

"The last I knew, a husband was sort of the usual way to get a baby. Or at least some guy in the direct picture."

"Usually," she agreed wryly. "Believe me, I haven't quit looking. But being a Fortune has a few disadvantages—a lot of guys were more interested in courting the family money than me. And sitting home writing books doesn't make for meeting a lot of new men, either. It just isn't that easy to find a white knight—or it hasn't been for me—and I've got a biological clock ticking loud and strong."

"I'll bet you *have* been prey to a lot of fortune hunters...but you're hardly ancient."

"Old enough. Thirty-three is a good, healthy age to have a child. And, thankfully, this is the nineties. No one's going to look sideways if I choose to be a single mom. This is an ideal time for me to have a baby—I'm ready, I'm healthy, I'm financially prepared to be a parent, and I'm dying for a baby. Or six."

Six? Gabe swallowed hard. "You don't think sperm banks are a little...drastic?"

"I think marrying the wrong man just because I'm hungry for a family would be "drastic." I'm sold on true love, cutie, and have absolutely no interest in settling for less. But I also want a family. Children to love and care for. For sure it'd be better if there was a loving dad in the picture, but if that's not in the cards, there's no reason I can't deal from another deck."

"Have you talked this out with your mama?"

"Kate?" Rebecca's grin was amused. "You think my mom would talk me out of this?"

Damn straight he did. Sperm banks, for God's sake!

"Well, I hate to disillusion you, darlin', but my mom would back me up all the way. She always has. From the day I was born, Kate encouraged me to take my own roads. I know on the surface no one sees us as alike—she's a hardheaded, practical businesswoman, a high-profile achiever. No accident that she's the head of a financial empire. I'm not like that, Gabe, never will be. But she pushed me toward writing, pushed me toward living my life on my own terms, my own way, and taught me never to back down from what I wanted and believed in. Believe me, my mom wouldn't give me any argument over this."

Somehow Gabe thought otherwise. Somehow he was damn sure Kate would like her youngest married off, preferably to a guy who could keep her impulsive baby safe and under control. Sperm banks didn't fit in that scenario, no way and nohow.

Rebecca's gaze roamed his face. Something in the way she probingly studied him aroused an uneasy feeling. "You don't have a male biological clock ticking of your own? No desire to have a son, a daughter, family to come home to at night? A new generation of Devereax?"

"The past generation of Devereax wasn't anything worth repeating," he said shortly. "I don't have your idealistic view about families. They only read great in storybooks."

"That's an awfully cynical view, cutie."

"Realistic," he corrected her, and abruptly leaned across her chest to open her car door. The whole personal nature of this conversation was crazy. It was past time to cut it off. "You go home, soak out those aches and bruises, get some sleep. Don't even think about that letter—I'll follow through with it. Stay out of it from now on, Rebecca."

"I'll be darned. Did you suddenly get elected my boss?"

Four in the morning, and she still had the energy to dish out grief. "Look, you came up with a lead. You did really good. You did more toward helping your brother than a whole team of people have done so far. But that letter also changes things, because it potentially—potentially—puts another suspect in the picture."

"So?"

"So, if there *is* another potential suspect, that person is also a potential murderer. And dammit, shorty, that's nothing to take lightly."

"Yes, Gabe."

"Even if this Tammy Diller had nothing to do with Monica's murder—something was wrong there. She doesn't sound like anyone you need to be messing with. You stay away from her. You hear me?"

"I sure do, cutie."

She pushed open the door and climbed out, but for a few moments she poked her head inside the darkened car and just looked at him. She'd been smiling before then. Smiling in a distracting, mischievous way that made him unsure how much she was putting him on and how much she was telling him straight.

But suddenly she wasn't smiling. This strange, warm, intense look shone from her eyes, making his pulse chug with alarm. For one horrifying moment, he was scared she was going to throw her arms around him again—and for damn sure, it was alarm that was chugging through his pulse, not anticipation.

"I know you don't believe this," she murmured, "but I'm a big girl and I can take care of myself. Get some sleep yourself, Gabe. And for sure don't waste your time worrying about me."

Not worry about her? Gabe watched her sprint toward the red Ciera—she dropped her backpack, picked it up, stubbed her toe when she almost tripped—and then finally made it into her car, which, he noted without surprise, wasn't locked. She didn't lock her door. She believed in love and white knights. As far as Gabe could tell, she really believed that right would prevail and nothing could hurt her.

And he wasn't supposed to worry about her?

Rebecca parked the rented Ford Taurus in the only spare spot she could find in three blocks, then gulped a breath as she peered out the window. It was incredibly warmer in Los Angeles than in the bitter March winds she'd left in Minnesota that morning. But she was really unfamiliar with this part of the city. Late-afternoon sun glinted on the Randolph Street sign. She was on the correct street. There was no way to park any closer to 12970, but she could walk the few blocks.

The neighborhood, though, left a tad to be desired. A cluster of tattooed skinheads were monopolizing one corner. Kids of all ages were hanging out in doorways. Graffiti spray-painted on all walled surfaces offered a free sex education. A man lay sprawled on the sidewalk, either dead or dead drunk; garbage spilled and reeked from rusty containers, and if she wasn't mistaken, this street was sort of owned by the Tigre gang...judging from the tough young fellas sporting that tag on their bandannas and Ts.

Boy, are you a long way from home, Toto. Gulping hard again, Rebecca stepped out of the car and locked it up tight, thinking that she'd written about scenes like this a zillion times...but never directly experienced one before. Through all the nuisance travel arrangements it took to get here, from the flight to L.A. to getting maps and renting a car, she'd considered that Gabe would probably have an eensy stroke if he knew she was here.

But then, Gabe had no reason to guess that she'd memorized Tammy Diller's address before giving him the letter…or that she'd be up at first light, putting travel plans in motion.

A hispanic boy—maybe twelve?—whistled when she walked past. He'd make a tempting father, she thought objectively. Not the child. Gabe. It was relatively more comforting to concentrate on Gabe than to have a heart attack over the blank-eyed guy flicking open his switchblade just off to her left.

Gabe was patient, principled, protective. Outstanding father qualities. No fortune hunter—or skinhead—would ever get near *his* daughter. As far as she could tell, Gabe didn't give a rat's tail about money, wasn't swayed by anyone with it—or without it. He'd teach a son or daughter the right values. She couldn't imagine him losing his temper. The only thing she'd ever caught annoying him was… well…her.

That kiss had lingered hard in her mind. It had been a lonely kiss. Hungry. Hot. Sexy. She'd always loved the idea of being blown away by a man's kisses, but it had never happened to her. Of course, the vast majority of her experience had been kissing frogs—fellas with their minds more on her family's money than on her—or nice guys who seemed to prefer their bathwater tepid. Not hot. Not risky. Not dangerous.

The delicious wickedness of that kiss had nothing to do with his having seriously good father potential…but, unfortunately, his attitude did. He'd never said why he was so antifamily. Actually she didn't know him well enough that they'd ever had a chance to talk about it. But his feelings had always been clear.

She wondered if he was equally dead set against playing a lover's role. With her. She wondered whether he'd be as thorough under the sheets as he was with his job. She wondered if he'd feel as hot, and make her feel as delectably, wantonly dangerous—and immoral—as the emotions he'd inspired so damn effortlessly with a few kisses.

She wondered if she'd lost her mind, to be thinking about sex and Gabe when six fellas—all wearing Tigre T-shirts—were walking shoulder-to-shoulder toward her. Even from twenty yards away, she could see the cold eyes, the strutting postures, the attitude. They were staring straight at her. And all the loitering bystanders who'd been milling all over the place seconds ago seemed to be scattering like leaves in the wind.

Possibly wearing a green silk dress and heels was a less-than-practical choice, but she'd had no way to know ahead of time what kind of neighborhood the address would be in. Whoever this Tammy Diller was, the woman knew Monica. Rebecca had never anticipated that any acquaintance of the ostentatious, image-obsessed Monica would be living in this kind of down-and-out neighborhood.

She'd assumed it would be a good idea to dress nice. Now she wished for running shoes instead of three-inch sucker heels. And a bulletproof vest instead of a short, thin dress. The charm bracelet jangled from her wrist, catching the bright L.A. sunlight, and probably the gold at her throat was a bit noticeable, too.

The six guys were closing in. One was definitely looking at her throat. One was definitely looking at her legs. All six of them certainly looked like an impenetrable wall. Throwing up was looming as an option. She wasn't sure if there were any statistics on whether throwing up discouraged thieves or murderers, but when Rebecca was scared enough, she was an excellent thrower-upper.

The tall one with the spiked black hair said something to one of his cronies. The sly whisper appeared to be about her, and set off a set of chuckles that rippled through the rest of them. Her stomach clenched in rope knots. They were within ten yards of her. Five. Forming a semicircle now, not just a wall.

She swallowed bile. Cocked up her chin, stocked up all the bravado she could muster and met the tall one's eyes with her best company smile. "Hi," she said cheerfully. "Could you help me?"

Perhaps the lad had never heard the words before. Perhaps none of them had, because all six of them seemed momentarily too startled to look tough. Then the tall, skinny one cocked a leg forward. "You bet I can help you, babe." His voice was low and rough, making the others laugh again.

If she'd worn her red shoes, maybe she could have tried clicking the heels three times in the hope of landing safely in Kansas. Bravado didn't seem to be getting her real far, but right then she seemed real short on other choices. "Well, good. That's just great," she said heartily. "Would you happen to know a woman named Tammy Diller? She lives in this neighborhood—" ducking her head, she reached for the piece of paper in her purse with the address on it "—at 12970 Randolph. Right up the next block from here?"

"Don't know no Tammy Diller. But I'd sure like to know you, babe. Real, real well." A hand covered with snake rings reached out, etched her collar with a long, slow fingertip.

Well, so much for fake courage. She was going to throw up on him, and there was absolutely nothing she could do about it.

Abruptly, though, he dropped his hand. Just as swiftly, the slow, insinuating smile on his face disappeared. He stepped back. Suddenly none of the six were smiling. They all stepped back.

Instinctively Rebecca whipped her head around. And there was Gabe, standing behind her as if he'd appeared out of nowhere. His scowl was darker than a tornado cloud. In fact, he looked mad enough to shred steel with a single glare.

Four

"Left without paying last month's rent, those two. I shoulda known better'n to believe them. The boyfriend—Wayne, Dwayne, something like that—he's a real looker, but ain't got that much upstairs. Tammy, now, she's the one could charm a fish into flying. Always dressed real nice, pretty eyes—a few miles of road on that face, but no man I ever met'd mind traveling a few more with her. The way those two looked, the way they dressed, I jes' believed what she said about their being temporary down on their luck. Shore didn't seem to belong in this neighborhood, otherwise—"

Gabe cut through this long monologue. The landlord had a face like a possum—long nose, beady eyes—but he was more talkative than a magpie. "So this Tammy Diller cut out on you. And her boyfriend, Dwayne or Wayne—?"

"I can't tell you his name for sure. She was the one paying me—and in cash, yet—so I didn't pay that much mind to the baggage she was carrying with her. Didn't like the boyfriend much, though, can tell you that. He smiled with too many white teeth. You ask me, never trust a man with a smile like—"

"When was the last time you saw them?"

"Mebbe two weeks ago. I keep good care of the building, mind you, but I ain't saying I'm here every day. Renters'll plague you about every little leaky faucet and light switch if you let 'em—"

"I'm sure they do," Gabe said consolingly. "So you haven't seen either of them in two weeks...and I don't suppose you have any idea where they might have gone?"

"If I had any idea where they'd gone, I'd be after them for the rent they owe me. Could be some of the neighbors know more, but I asked them, got nowhere. Course, people in this neighborhood ain't much on talking...."

The landlord was clearly an exception to that rule. As long as the man came up with information on Tammy Diller, Gabe could keep a rein on his impatience, but that abruptly changed. Instinctively he reached a hand behind him. He expected to connect with a body. He connected with nothing but air.

Tuning out the landlord entirely, he whipped his head around. A millisecond before, Rebecca had been at his side—and definitely close enough to grab. Now she was gone.

When he got her alone, he planned to kill her—preferably a nice physical death, like strangling her with his bare hands. If anyone was going to do her harm, though, he wanted first dibs. Which meant keeping her safe until he had the privilege, and in this neighborhood that meant keeping her in sight, and preferably on a short, tight leash.

Gabe escaped from the gregarious landlord and hiked straight for the sagging screen door. It banged behind him. A cinch she wouldn't stay inside, where she was relatively safe—Rebecca didn't have the brains of a bat, much less any functioning self-protective instincts.

Outside, it was hot, muggy and airless. He paused for ten fast seconds, scanning anything that moved for any glimpse of a redhead. No question she'd stand out in this crowd. A hooker in a tight black leather skirt was soliciting on the far corner, a drug deal going down half a dozen yards from her. A scrawny kid raced past, nearly tripping over Gabe, a nude magazine clutched to his chest and a wizened, whiskery storekeeper shouting after him.

When Gabe arrived from Minnesota that afternoon—in damn good travel time, mind you—he'd known exactly what kind of street Tammy Diller lived on. He'd expected to find every single thing he saw when he climbed out of his car—except Rebecca, scared out of her tree, surrounded by a half-dozen punks. The image replaying in his mind made his blood pressure rise all over again.

If she'd gotten herself in more trouble, he really was going to kill her. And, dammit, she'd better not be hurt. Now where the *hell* could she have gone—?

There. He caught sight of the bobbing head, the

lush russet-auburn hair glinting fire in the fading sun. Her body had been blocked for a few seconds...by a black dude about six feet five inches tall, in a muscle T, hair shaved in an initial on his scalp and shoulders flexing his tattoos. Rebecca was apparently talking to him. Willingly—as if she were having a happy chat with a good ol' boy.

From behind, Gabe could see that the dude had a seven-inch blade slugged in his back pocket. When she shifted on those damn silly high heels, Gabe had a clear view of her tousled hair, the bandaged gash on her forehead, the fanny-hugging short dress and the expensive gold glittering at her bare throat and wrists. The dude turned his head, too, and Gabe saw the long knife scar on the fella's face. The guy lifted his hand toward her.

Gabe didn't take time to swear. And he'd moved faster. Just not in the past decade. There were too many people milling the streets for him to outright run, but when strangers caught the expression on his face, they promptly gave him clearance. Her auburn head kept dipping out of sight, but the tall black dude was an easy landmark.

His lungs were chugging hard and his veins mainlining adrenaline by the time he came up behind the guy. His instinctive response was to grab the guy's arm. Mr. Muscle-bound yanked around with a growled *"Hey!"*

When Rebecca spotted him, her response was an

instant "Gabe! Guess what?" in a voice more laden with guileless delight than Pollyanna's.

In three seconds flat, Gabe realized that the dude hadn't been lifting a hand to harm Rebecca, but to shake hers. He let the guy go and tried to cool down. She wouldn't recognize danger if it bit her on the tush, but for reasons beyond all logic in life—and especially this neighborhood—she wasn't in danger. She bubbled out that this was Snark, and could he believe it, Snark knew Tammy, and the last Snark heard, Tammy and her boyfriend had taken off for Las Vegas, claimed to have some "business" there.

Snark eyed him with all the friendliness of a cobra—he knew damn well why Gabe had grabbed his arm—but any body language or eye contact flew right over Rebecca's head. Snark settled down. So did Gabe's blood pressure. Eventually.

And eventually her delightful new friend ambled off in a strutting stride down the street, leaving him alone with Ms. Bubbly Green Eyes.

"So we might not have caught up with them, but at least we have another lead on where Tammy has gone now. Did you pick up any other information?"

"No," Gabe said curtly.

"Well—" Rebecca seemed to be trying to sound empathetic "—sometimes a woman just has an easier way of getting people to talk. Good thing I came, hmm?"

She *had* picked up information that he hadn't. That her investigative techniques could have gotten her killed—or worse—didn't seem to occur to her. Gabe hooked an arm under her elbow. The way she looked, she was drawing attention from any male eye within a three-block radius—and the damn woman didn't seem to realize that, either. *"Where* is your car?"

"A couple blocks down." She motioned vaguely. With her left hand. He noticed she didn't jerk her right arm away from his, although there was a sudden, interesting flush of color on her cheeks.

"I'm walking you there." His tone dared her to argue. "And then where are you staying?"

"I haven't made motel arrangements yet. It was all I could do to get a flight out this morning and get all that travel stuff done. I just figured when I got here, I'd worry about motels and a place to stay."

Gabe suspected that "worry" was a vast exaggeration on her part. Put her in a nest of vipers, and Rebecca probably wouldn't worry. He told himself for the dozenth time that it wasn't her fault she'd come from such a sheltered, protected background— and it wasn't. But trying to keep such a rabid idealist safe was a mite on the challenging side.

"You know your way around the city?"

"I've been to L.A. all kinds of times." She paused. "Although not exactly around here. I have a map, though—"

"Uh-huh. I'll drive with you to my car. Then you follow me, shorty, until we get you set up somewhere for the night."

The Shelton Arms wasn't the Ritz, Rebecca mused, but it had all the comforts that would appeal to a man. The T-bone brought up by room service was definitely marine-size. The armchair was huge enough for a woman to curl up and nap in, and the room colors were all subdued blue tones.

Rebecca finished her T-bone, and a mountainous baked potato and a Caesar salad, then peeked under the lid at Gabe's plate. "If you don't want your prime rib..." she warned him.

"I'm coming, I'm coming."

"Before we've even kissed? That's amazing."

Gabe sighed, heavily and loudly. "Anyone ever tell you you've got a dangerous set of humor, Red? And get your hands off my prime rib."

"You were concentrating so hard, I didn't think you'd notice." Long before room service arrived, Gabe had set up a laptop on the far desk. The gumshoe era had definitely died, Rebecca mused. Gabe didn't have to walk anywhere—even through the yellow pages—to plug into a zillion data bases for information. "Well? Did you find out if our dear Tammy knocked up any traceable credit charges in Las Vegas?"

"Yup. She's there. Charges all on her, none on the boyfriend, so I can't tell if he's with her. Could be that he depleted his credit a long time ago. Or that she took off solo from him. And I strongly suspect that 'Tammy Diller' is a made-up name, because the whole credit record on her has a short life history. A fake name would be a handy way for her to reinvent herself when credit sources dried up.''

"And a fake name would make it extrahard to track her down...but from the charges in Vegas, could you find out where she was staying?''

"Yeah." But he neglected to tell her where, just lurched out of that chair and stretched, rolling his shoulders, before ambling over to the room service tray. "You actually leveled that entire plate of food?''

"My theory on cholesterol is that if you're gonna do something bad, you might as well binge and do it right.''

"You'll never finish that hot fudge sundae,'' he predicted.

Her eyes danced. "Ah, Gabe. Clearly you don't know me at all well. Nothing, cutie—not tornadoes, world wars, or an audit by the IRS—would ever get between me and my chocolate.'' She'd long ago kicked off her heels, but now she curled up with her legs under her and settled back in the armchair with the sundae and a spoon.

Gabe dug in, conquering his prime rib with the same thoroughness and efficiency with which he did everything else. No taking time to savor. No taking time to smell the roses. Food was a body-mainte- nance requirement. A job was a job.

Even as he devoured dinner, though, his eyes were on her. She thought he might be just a teensy bit afraid she'd swing from the chandeliers at any time if he didn't watch her—even though the room didn't have any chandeliers. Her room was down the hall from his. No chandeliers there, either. Gabe had set her up in the same hotel he was staying at, specifically in a room on the same floor, and then suggested they have dinner together via room service. With any other man, she'd at least have considered that he might want to make something of that situation.

Gabe rolled his eyes as she spooned in another gooey mouthful, and she thought, No. If Gabe even remembered they'd shared a kiss hot enough to cause spontaneous combustion, it didn't show. He was treating her no different than if she were a pesky younger sister—with chicken pox.

When he finished eating, he crossed over to the locked minibar by the bed, turned the key and pulled out a tiny bottle of Scotch. "Do you want anything to drink?"

"I'd love a glass of wine, if it's in there," she admitted.

"Wine? On top of a hot fudge sundae?" He shuddered.

"I've got a cast-iron stomach. More to the point, I'm afraid if I have coffee, I'll be too keyed up to sleep. But it's no big deal, if there's no wine in there—"

"There is." He rummaged around in the extravagant goodies and pulled out a wine carafe, about large enough to hold two glasses' worth. "I have no idea if it's any good, though."

"Doesn't matter. Coming from the Fortune family, you'd think I'd know the difference between a screwtop and a cork quality of wine. But all any alcohol does is make me sleepy," she admitted wryly. "Gabe...what do you think is the connection between Monica Malone and this Tammy?"

"So far, I haven't found one. Monica had a long history of going after whatever she wanted, by fair means or foul, so her tie to this woman could be anything. But I admit I've wondered if their relationship was somehow linked to your family."

Rebecca blinked. "You think that's likely?"

"I think the one consistent thread in Monica's life was a long, personal vendetta against your family. She was obsessed with your father for years, to the point of kidnapping his son when she couldn't have a child by him herself. She was behind the theft of the secret youth formula—we know she hired people to break into the lab, know she was actively involved in Allie's stalker. There just sems no limit to her neurotic obsession and jealousy of your family."

"Then your brother is accused of murder where this woman's name suddenly pops up...it seems like a lot of coincidences. But so far I know of no tie. From the computer records we've picked up so far, I'd guess this Tammy is pretty familiar with living on the edge. Her name shows up out of nowhere, yet there's no employment record, no steady address, and somehow she's coming up with sudden influxes of money and credit. Reads like the résumé of a scam artist to me.''

"That would make sense. Especially considering the contents of that letter. Something had Monica ticked off. Maybe this Tammy was trying to blackmail her about something. And darn it, something about her name keeps ringing bells for me, but I can't place what it is.''

"Well, I've got staff working on the Tammy Diller name at home. Her past will surface. It always does. Secrets never stay buried, especially if they're dirty ones. It just may take some time to come up with more information.''

And time was the one thing they were short of, Rebecca thought. She plopped the empty sundae bowl on the serving tray and curled back up with her wineglass. "So...when are we going to Las Vegas?''

"*We* aren't going anywhere, shorty.''

"Hey! Did I find the clue leading us to Tammy? Did I find the next lead locating her in Las Vegas? Hello? Did anyone notice I've been more than a little useful so far? Speaking for myself, love bug, I can travel alone. But it seems pretty silly not to team up, when we're both trying to dig up the same information.''

Gabe poured the Scotch into the hotel's water glass and slugged it down, his eyes on her face like a blanket on a bed. "This Tammy may not have a criminal record, but everything I've picked up on her so far indicates she's just been lucky about not getting caught. She's fishier than a trout, Red.''

"Yeah? So what's your point? Technically, that's good news—or least helpful news. She sounds more and more like a serious suspect in Monica's murder to me, even if we don't have hard facts yet.''

"The point,'' Gabe said in his patient-maestro voice, ''is that I want you to go home. I think she's bad news. And I think if there's the slightest prayer she's involved in Monica's murder, she isn't going to appreciate anyone asking questions or poking in her past. You'd be better off going home and concentrating on book-writing and babies.''

"I would…in fact, I'd be thrilled to do just that…if my brother weren't still sitting in a jail cell.'' Quietly she set down the wineglass. She'd expected this lecture, figured he'd never have invited her in for dinner—with him, alone—if he didn't feel obligated to have this private talk. She struggled again to honestly explain her feelings to him. "Gabe, I was petrified this afternoon. Scared of everything I saw on Randolph Street. Scared of Snark, and yeah, that was going okay, but don't think I didn't appreciate your showing up when you did. I was in way, way over my head.''

"Dammit, red, that's exactly what I've been trying to tell you.''

She nodded…and then gently, firmly, continued. "But Jake is my brother. He's family. And I don't care what I have to do—or what I'm scared of. Until his name is cleared, there is nothing and no one that could keep me from trying to help him.''

Gabe listened, she mused. He just didn't seem to get it. A strange, silvery-soft feeling clutched at her heart as she thoughtfully studied him. She cared about him. Personally cared, in a way that had nothing to do with her brother, nothing to do with the odd "bedmates" they made as far as working together. Before, of course, she never had a chance to really get to know him.

He was tired, she realized. Those dramatic dark eyes seemed almost hauntingly black when he was exhausted. It was the first time she'd ever seen him even close to relaxed, sprawled in a chair, his hair rumpled, his chin with a shadow of whiskers. Even when he was dead beat, that jaw had a stubborn thrust—he was undoubtedly marshaling another argument to convince her to leave. She tried another tack—she hungered to learn more about him, anyway. "Gabe, you don't have a brother yourself? Or family that you feel that way about?"

He answered her easily enough. "I have family. I just grew up in a different world than you did. I came from the rough side of New Orleans. My parents fought like pit bulls. My oldest brother took the road of petty crime. The next one split from home as soon as he could, and never came back. I escaped by joining the army. From everything I saw growing up, people who claim to love each other do more to destroy than any battle scenes I've ever been part of—

and I've been part of a few. So, no. I don't have family I 'feel that way' about.''

"I'm sorry," she said softly.

He looked startled at her response. "Nothing to be sorry about."

Rebecca thought there was. She'd often brought up babies because it was such a predictable way to get a rise out of Gabe. From the start, they'd bantered and bickered about her idealism versus his "more realistic" view of life. Teasing him for being such a hard-core cynic was fun...but she hadn't known about his upbringing before. It sounded loveless and harsh and lonely.

She'd always believed in love and family and children, and, yeah, even in the core goodness of mankind. She had never considered her values idealistic or altruistic, but simply the gut core of everything that mattered in life. And she couldn't help aching for Gabe, who'd been deprived of them.

"Now what are you looking at me like that for?" he asked suspiciously.

"No reason. I was just wondering if you hadn't found someone to love in all this time."

"I've found plenty to love, shorty. I just never had rose-colored glasses about expecting any kind of 'romantic love' to last. Life's treated me damn well. I never needed illusions to make it prettier." He abruptly frowned, as if he were confounded by how the conversation had gotten sidetracked in such an irrelevant direction. "Back to the subject of your going home on the next flight out—"

She uncoiled from the chair and stood up. The effect of the long day—and that huge dinner—suddenly hit her with the power of a sedative. She'd snatched only a few hours' sleep in the past forty-eight hours, and bruises and stress were making her feel more battered than a whipped dog.

"Now, Gabe," she said lightly, "Don't get your liver in an uproar, but I'm not taking the first flight out tomorrow—going anywhere. As fast as my head hits a pillow, I plan to be comatose for the next twelve hours."

He lurched out of his chair, too, so swiftly that she suspected he was downright thrilled to end this tête-à-tête. "Sleep's a good idea. You really look whipped."

"Please. I can't take any more extravagant compliments. They go straight to my head."

The devil had an unrepentant grin. "I wasn't insulting you—"

She corrected him dryly. "You're *always* insulting me."

"Well, you *do* look tired. And I think the only thing that went straight to your head was that half glass of wine. Where'd you put your shoes? And have you got your room key?"

"They're around here somewhere." She glanced around, but somehow ended up searching his face instead of the room. Somehow, before, she'd mistaken the depths in those dark eyes for coldness, instead of loneliness. Gabe believed in honor, responsibility, duty. Even when he was weary, his posture was contained, formal, and as rigid as a soldier's, reflecting the values he'd found in life to sustain him. He'd found values. It just didn't sound to Rebecca as if he'd ever found love.

She meant to bend down to pick up her shoes, and yet somehow found her arms raising up instead of going down. Because he'd plucked her room key from the table to hand it to her, he was physically close at that instant. Close enough to hug, and the impulse to hug him was suddenly irresistible. Her heart lined up a set of fine excuses. She hated to think about his growing up, trapped in such an angry and lonely and violent environment. And even if he drove her nuts with his chauvinistic tendency to protect any woman in his path, he'd been there for her over the past few days. And…

Well, damn. None of those reasons were more than spinning wheels. She needed to hug him. There was really nothing more complicated about it than that.

Two seconds after she wrapped her arms around his neck, the room's air-conditioning suffered a massive malfunction. The temperature rose at least thirty degrees. The tropics couldn't be any hotter than the heat spontaneously combusting between them. It couldn't possibly have been generated by her. She'd never intended anything but an innocent, impulsive, instinctive hug.

When his mouth latched on to hers, fused on hers, all innocent thoughts scattered like wind. Nothing innocent could possibly be this much fun. Or this much danger.

She wasn't precisely sure how a hug turned into a kiss. She definitely couldn't analyze what happened after that. He tasted like that warm Scotch—not nice, not sweet, but tangy and potent and heady. She tasted a slam of hunger. She tasted a man trying to warn her, thoroughly and explicitly, that a grown man never anted in a poker game for anything as tame as kisses...and she was sure as hell old enough to know better than to tease a tiger.

She wasn't teasing. Maybe she should have remembered the drowning-danger sensation from their first embrace, but this was so different. Maybe no one had kissed this tiger in a long time—at least not a kiss with caring and emotion invested in it—because her Gabe just seemed to explode. Not with roughness. But with responsive need.

His hands roamed her sides and back, clutching, stroking, sliding over the silk of her dress as if he could inhale her closer to him. Her breasts crushed against his harder chest, molding against his contours. He smelled like hot sun and a wild natural wind and like soap that swept clean any illusions she'd had about men before. Gabe was like no other man she'd ever known. Her feelings were like nothing she'd ever experienced.

She'd never had a submissive bone in her whole body, yet this yielding feeling wasn't like submitting. It was like belonging, like her bones were supposed to turn liquid for Gabe, like all the strength she valued in herself as a woman was important...but not with him.

One of his hands climbed up, tangled and fisted in her hair. She tasted his tongue. Her neck began to ache from the pressure of his kisses, yet his tongue was like wet velvet, intimate, seeking, treasuring the dark secrets he found in her mouth. Somewhere she heard a faucet dripping. Somewhere she saw city lights flash from a slit in the curtains. Somewhere she felt his arousal, pulsing, alive, growing hard and hot against her abdomen.

She couldn't breathe. Didn't want to. This wasn't wrong. Her whole life, she'd trusted her instincts over facts. Her whole life, she'd believed when an instinct promised her that something was right. Heat surged through her veins, and desire more powerful than she was prepared for or understood, yet her thundering heart kept making her the insane promise that it was okay, with Gabe, that even admitting to fear was right with him.

His hands roamed, caressing, claiming and learning her through the slippery silk fabric, roamed farther down. He cupped her fanny, ground her into him intimately, the caress more intimate, more bluntly sexual, than...

She yelped. Undoubtedly startling herself more than him.The yelp was certainly no sensible objection to how fast this forest fire was spinning way, way out of her control. But she had a mortifying-size bruise on her fanny, from the fall in Monica's house. And when he pressed on that spot, she couldn't stop her involuntary response.

Gabe reared back. "I hurt you?"

"No. That is, yes. But not like you're thinking." There were so many lush sensations swirling in her mind that she couldn't seem to say anything coherent. "I'm fine. You just accidentally touched a bruise."

"I just deliberately touched a hell of a lot more than a bruise." And he dropped his hands faster than if he'd been handling hot potatoes. His voice was hoarse, his breathing labored, and the look in his eyes was pure black fire. "Dammit, Rebecca."

"Dammit, Gabe," she echoed, but her voice was soft. She wanted to make him smile. "You're one heck of a kisser, love bug. Don't blame me for enjoying it."

"I'm not blaming you for anything. Neither of us asked for the chemistry. I just think we both know that letting this go any farther—or happen again—is a real bad idea."

"We're not exactly alike," she murmured.

"We have as much in common as a butterfly and a rock." Swiftly he located her room key again, wrapped her fist around it, then forced the straps of her heels in her other hand. "I'm walking you to your room," he said curtly.

He walked her to her room and saw her inside, with no conversation and a dark gloom of a scowl that warned her away from trying any. Once inside, she tossed her shoes and key on the bed, then leaned back against the closed door and let loose an uneasy and rattling-huge sigh.

Gabe was right about their having nothing in common. His reasons for being antifamily were clearer now, but understanding his background didn't change anything. She wanted babies. She wanted a family. She wanted real love—or nothing—and there was no purpose in involving herself with a man who didn't value families and commitment as she did.

Yet her body was still shivery, still alive and awake, from those wild, wanton kisses with him. Her pulse was still racing; her knees still felt liquid.

Maybe it was just sex. Maybe she was so shook up only because she'd never had a man charge her hormones anything like this before. And Gabe had persisted in being bluntly honest with her. He was the wrong man for her to get involved with.

But that didn't make these winsome, wild feelings disappear. And until her brother's name was cleared, spending more time with Gabe was inevitable. Re-

becca couldn't remember ever feeling so lost and unsure. She was painfully afraid that she could get over
her head real, real quickly with Gabe, unless she was
very careful.

Five

Some might find the situation ironic, Gabe thought. He'd wanted Rebecca on the first flight leaving home for Minnesota, and instead, he was the one on that flight—alone.

Dawn was just peeking over the horizon when he exited the airport in Minneapolis–St. Paul, lugging his laptop and a travel tote, his mood full of spit and vinegar. He never needed much sleep, and the catnap on the flight had revived him. He'd considered waking Rebecca when he made the travel arrangements, but she'd been so exhausted that he strongly suspected she would snooze the clock around. She was safe enough in that L.A. hotel. He'd slipped a note under the door so that she'd know he was gone, but *where* was definitely none of that redhead's business.

It was her mama's business, though.

Less than an hour later, he'd retrieved his black Lexus—no way he'd have abandoned his antique Morgan in a riffraff airport parking lot—copped some fast-food breakfast, and was winging through the lobby of the Fortune Cosmetics offices. A security guard cleared his ID before allowing him access to the private elevator—the one shooting up to the floor with the testing labs, and Kate Fortune's personal office.

Technically, Jake Fortune was paying the bills for this investigation job, and while Jake was being held without bail for this murder charge, the checks were signed by Sterling Foster, the family retainer. Gabe was expected to report information and results to both of them. And did. But working with the Fortunes was never simple, and Gabe always understood who held the real power and control cards in the family.

Kate Fortune expected to know anything and everything that affected her offspring. She preferred regular face-to-face contact, couldn't stand phones, and if that was an inconvenient nuisance, she paid handsomely for the expense of having things done her way. Gabe would have catered to her, expenses or no expenses.

He liked her. His first contact with the Fortune family had been to investigate Kate's death—her plane had gone down in the jungle when a hijacker tried to take over. A body had been found and everyone had assumed it was Kate's, but she had been thrown from the wreckage and rescued by a South American tribe. When she'd recovered she'd slowly made her way back to Minneapolis—just in time for the reading of her will. She'd been afraid the attacker would try to kill her again or use her family against her if she revealed herself to them so she had only contacted Sterling Foster, the family lawyer and an old friend. She'd spent the next few years watching her family from afar and doing a little matchmaking. But there was no way she'd let her eldest son be accused of murder without being there to support him.

From their first meeting, she'd won both Gabe's admiration and his respect. And despite certain similar personality traits in her daughter, Kate Fortune was a reasonable, rational straight shooter of a woman, easy to be around, because a man knew just where he stood with her.

Surprising him not at all, Kate was running on a full head of steam even at 7:00 a.m., and had coffee poured before he even sat down. Considering that she was the owner of a cosmetics empire, her new office—she hadn't made everyone rearrange themselves upon her return—was distinctly all business and no froufrou. The walls were teak and the carpet was a luxurious Oriental, but the desk and furniture were no-nonsense, and Kate was wearing a practical lab coat.

"How long have you been up and working?" he asked her.

She chuckled. "What I do is play, not work, Gabe…and I've been here since five. I love the early-morning hours. No phones, no interruptions. You can't get anything *good* done during normal business hours." She propped a pair of gold-rimmed glasses on her nose. Typically, she wasted no time. "So what do you have for me?"

He filled her in on every lead he'd tried—both the blind alleys and the successes. When he handed her the copy of Monica's letter to Tammy Diller, he saw her forehead pinch in a perplexed frown. It didn't take her long to read the short letter, but it was long enough for him to study her.

Rebecca looked amazingly like her mama. To a point. Kate had had her youngest late in life, but had to be in her late sixties now. They were both built lithe and slim, with the same elegant bone structure. Both had the same unforgettable eyes and the same lustrous, luxuriant auburn hair—but Kate's had streaks of steel, matching all the gutsy steel in her personality, and she wore it neatly pinned up, like the no-nonsense businesswoman she was.

Kate surely used some of the cosmetics her company had made famous, but there was nothing painted about her. Even in morning sunlight, her face had few lines—and those she didn't hide. Kate was unsentimental, strong. She had a hell of a cocky, authoritarian air, but that was precisely why Gabe had taken to her from the first. She was a shrewd, sharp woman of principle. She backed down for nobody. As far as Gabe was concerned, she'd earned the right to be bossy, and she had the devil's own dry sense of humor, which tickled his own.

Gabe couldn't look at the mama—the bones, the elegance, the sassy humor, the never-back-down-on-a-principle temperament—and fail to think of Rebecca. But a man could *talk* to Kate. The mama took her realism straight, no chaser. Gabe wasn't sure the daughter could recognize the word in a big-print dictionary with a magnifying glass.

Kate finished reading the letter, and handed it back to him. "This sure isn't much to clear my son of a murder charge. I'd hoped for more, Gabe."

"I'd hoped to have more for you—but there has to be dirt in order to find it." He'd never tried to soft-soap Kate. He'd never had to.

"I know." She leaned against the desk, facing his eyes squarely. "I can't swear that my son is innocent. I told you that at the start. But I want the truth— every ounce of evidence leading to the truth—no matter what it is. And with the trial imminent, the frightening problem is time. We need answers *now*. Every day that passes puts my son's case in even more jeopardy." She hesitated, staring out the window for a long minute before turning back to him. "That Tammy Diller's name really bothers me."

"Yeah. I saw you frown when you read the letter. I was hoping you might have recognized the name."

"Actually, I never heard of a Tammy Diller. It just startled me how similar the initials and name were to Tracey Ducet's." Kate lifted her hand in a helpless gesture. "Probably the similarity is just incidental, or coincidence. Heaven knows, I'm so worried about my son that I'm inclined to grasp at any straw. But the name popped so quickly into my mind because Ms. Ducet stirred a kettleful of problems for the family, then conveniently disappeared before we could nail her with any specifics. Do you know the story?''

''Yeah. I ran some background checks on Tracey Ducet when she first arrived and claimed to be the missing Fortune heir. But since Tracey didn't hang around for all that long and had no real proof of her claims, I had no reason to pay much attention and never really got the full story. Why don't you just tell me the whole thing?''

As restless as her daughter, Kate prowled and paced around her office with far too much energy to sit still. ''As you know, I've built an empire here— and there are always leeches and parasites hoping to prey on big money. Anyone who walks in these shoes has to expect those kinds of problems. Tracey Ducet was just one of the gnats. She was a hustler, a con artist...'' She hesitated again. ''I hate to waste your time with this. I really have no logical reason to think there could be a connection between that Tammy Diller woman and Tracey...''

''And maybe there isn't. But how about if you just spill out the story, and between the two of us, we can decide if it could possibly be relevant or not?''

Kate sighed. ''You already know that I had twins years ago, and that one of those babies was kidnapped. The press had such a field day with the kidnapping story that even years later, we occasionally got people claiming to be the missing heir. And that's how Tracey came into the picture—she got the idea she could pass herself off as the missing Fortune.

Undoubtedly the reason she believed she could pull it off was because of her looks. She amazingly resembles my daughter Lindsay—I mean, take out the gum and put her in decent clothes, and she could be Lindsay's mirror image.''

''But you knew that wasn't possible?'' Gabe asked.

''Unquestionably. The thing was, the FBI guarded information during the kidnapping investigation, in the hopes that we would catch the kidnapper. One of the details the media never exposed was that the missing twin was a boy, Brandon. There was just no way she could have pulled off this scam. Not on me. The rest of the family might have believed her—we tried to keep it quiet for them, and they knew that I had brought home Lindsay, but even they didn't know about the boy. I just couldn't face talking about it.''

But then Tracey disappeared before anything happened—it never came to pressing charges, nothing. She never actually broke any laws. I mean—she could have been an innocent miss who saw a picture of Lindsay and really thought she might be the missing heir.''

''From how you're describing her, it doesn't sound as if there's anything 'innocent' about Ms. Ducet,'' Gabe said dryly.

''I think she's a born tramp,'' Kate said, just as bluntly.

''And I'll put her in the computer, Kate, but I

don't want you to get your hopes up. Offhand, it doesn't sound real likely that both women could somehow have a connection to Monica Malone's murder.''

"No, I don't see how they could, either.''

Gabe scratched his chin. "Well, obviously she knew something, if the two were communicating. And if she found out Monica was involved in that kidnapping, Ms. Ducet might have smelled some easy money another way. Blackmail money.''

Kate looked heartened, but only for a moment. "This is all hopeful supposition, but I don't know how you could possibly prove it. And I'd like to believe it makes a difference, but I'm not so sure, Gabe. Even if the little tramp was involved in a blackmail scheme, unless we can come up with evidence that she had opportunity and a motive for murder, it won't help clear my son of this murder charge. You know, I thought there was something suspicious about her disappearance last year—remember when I 'appeared' at that seance last year? And I know the police had a witness who saw someone looking like Lindsay, but in the excitement of getting my life back and without proof or knowledge of her whereabouts it got pushed to the side.''

Gabe took a long look at her face. "Listen, please. I know you're worried, but keep in mind that we don't have to prove who killed Monica. We only have to prove that there's another viable suspect in the picture to win reasonable doubt for your son. And this Tammy Diller still looks like a winning bet to me. She's covered her past history damn well, but we've still got the letter, that connection to Monica, and we know where she is right now. In fact, I'm headed to Las Vegas after I leave here. And if there's anything to find on her, I'll find it." He hesitated. "There's a separate problem that I need to discuss with you."

Kate nodded, as if anticipating what he was going to say. "Transportation, of course. You'll get there faster with the company jet. I should have suggested it immediately—"

"No, it's not that. I've already got the tickets. I can handle my own transportation. Rebecca's the problem I wanted to talk with you about."

"Rebecca?" Kate peered at him over the rim of her gold-framed glasses. "How on earth did my daughter get in this conversation?"

Gabe had never been good with tact. One of the best parts of dealing with Kate was that he didn't have to be. "Your youngest has taken up breaking and entering, burglary, and chatting up gang members in inner-city neighborhoods—that's how." He frowned. "She's a little on the loyal side, where her brother is concerned."

Kate's restless pacing immediately stopped. She leaned against the desk and studied Gabe's face. Something in that thundercloud scowl and those dark eyes alerted all her maternal instincts. Right now, her oldest son was in desperate trouble, but that didn't mean she loved her other children any less. Her heart had a lot of room. And her youngest, although no one else had ever really seen it, was just like her. "Loyalty is one of those nasty Fortune Family traits, I know. And Rebecca always did have it badly."

"*Badly* doesn't begin to cut it. She thinks she's qualified to conduct an investigation. More to the point, she thinks she needs to be involved. I don't know if you've noticed, but Rebecca has a reckless streak. She's about as manageable as a volcano." Gabe lanced out of the chair as if a bee just stung his behind. "I figure if anyone has control over her, it's you. Call her off, Kate."

"Oh, dear," Kate murmured. Her shrewd eyes never left Gabe's face. "I'm afraid I've never had any control over Rebecca. In fact, I don't think anyone does."

"Well, someone has to." Gabe dug out his car keys. He was leaving in a minute, and the keys gave him something to clench in a fist. "I wouldn't tell her where this Tammy Diller was staying in Las Vegas. But I'm still afraid she'll fly there and try poking around. Not to offend you, Kate, but your daughter doesn't have the common sense of a cotton ball."

"I can see she's causing you a problem." Kate tried to sound sympathetic. It wouldn't do to sound amused. She'd been watching Gabe from the sidelines for a number of years and had seen Gabe in a number of crisis situations before, seen his responses to danger, stress, pressure. Nothing had ever rattled him before. It was most interesting to recognize that her youngest, her sweetest, the most softhearted of the whole family, had.

"Isn't there some nice guy in the picture? Somebody who has sway over her? Somebody who could sweet-talk her into listening?"

"Well, truthfully, there've been a number of very nice men. She never seems to let them any closer than first base. I've been worried for a long time that nice men just don't seem to be her cuppa. She's the only one of my brood who hasn't married. Believe me, I'd love to see her settled, but she seems to be..."

When Kate seemed to pause for the right words, Gabe obligingly filled in some of the obvious options. "Picky? Impossible? Bullheaded? Stubborn?"

"Hmm... I can see you *have* spent some time with her. Gabe?" She could see him clenching and unclenching those keys, and starting to move toward the door.

"What?"

There was no smile in Kate's voice now—or in her heart. "I don't give a damn what you have to do. Keep her safe. Don't let anything happen to her. I'm counting on you."

Swell, Gabe thought as his stomach dropped on the elevator ride a minute or two later. There was, of course, every chance that Rebecca wouldn't be so stupid and foolhardy as to head for Las Vegas. But he'd counted on her mama as an ally, and somehow ended up with another responsibility on his plate instead.

So far there was only a jumble of puzzle pieces in Monica's murder, but nothing seemed to be coming together. Kate's filling him in on the old Tracey Ducet history had pinned down another Fortune family enemy, but a family with that much money invariably collected enemies. The problem he needed to concentrate on was finding a direct link between Tammy Diller and Monica's murder. The letter implied a blackmail scheme to him, had from the first, and the difficulty in tracing Tammy's history implied the woman had something to hide. The whole thing smelled like trouble to Gabe. And where there was trouble, there was potential danger.

Keeping Rebecca safe from danger would only complicate an already complicated job. With or without her mama's mandate, though, Gabe would have done that.

Keeping that redhead safe from *him* was another dimension entirely. She did something, when her arms were around him, that stripped his mind bare. Hormones were just hormones, but there was something about that woman that shook his stable moorings.

On the other hand, Gabe wasn't one to borrow or imagine problems. Rebecca might be a rabid idealist, but she surely had an ounce of common sense stashed somewhere. If she had any functioning brains, she was en route home right now, and nowhere near Las Vegas.

Rebecca had barely stepped off the plane in Las Vegas before she heard the clink and clank of slot machines. Weary travelers gushed toward them, recharged by the first sound and sight of gambling.

She was tempted to empty out the quarters in her change purse and give the slot machines a try. Gambling was certainly in her blood. The Fortunes had always played for big stakes in business. Her mom believed that every reward worth having in life took risk, and cowards never had a chance at the brass ring.

Somehow, though, when she thought of gambling, slot machines and roulette wheels seemed to pale compared to Gabe. That man was a terrible risk, Rebecca mused. A woman would have to risk one heck of an ante to even play the game, and those were unknown stakes for an uncertain reward.

The thought blurred. Her stomach was grumbling, and her head was throbbing with a headache. She hadn't brushed her hair in hours, and she was wearing a teddy-bear sweatshirt that had to look as rumpled as she was.

Her brother needed to be on her mind, not Gabe, not anyone else. One way or another, she planned to find this Tammy Diller. But not until she'd had some real food—preferably a Big Mac and fries—and found someplace to stay. She'd been up since Gabe slipped the note under her door in the middle of the night—because she'd been too ticked off at him to sleep after that.

He'd left. In itself, that had been no surprise, and it had been reasonably polite of him to let her know he'd taken a powder. But the Neanderthal had ordered her to go home in the note. There was some indecipherable scribble about her being *safe*. She wouldn't put it past that blockheaded, overprotective, macho caveman jerk to sic her mom on her.

If Gabe had worried her mother, she'd have to kill him.

Thoughts of plots involving violent revenge revived her. So did the cab ride through town. She'd been in Paris, Switzerland, traveled the country with her family on various business trips and vacations. Vegas definitely had its own unique personality— endless neon and flashing glitter, women walking the sidewalks dressed in everything from red satin to torn jeans. Posters on street lamps advertised legal brothels. Rebecca gaped and gawked, as happy as any tourist.

"You got no reservations?" the cab driver queried her.

"No." She hadn't thought that far ahead. "Is that a problem?"

"You want to gamble, babe, ain't nothing a problem in this town." He'd already stopped for a Big Mac for her. Hey, it was the lady's dollar; she wanted to pay to sit in a fast-food line, it was okay by him. "But it'd be nice if you'd give me some idea of a destination here. You wanna stay downtown, or someplace on the strip?"

By the time he dropped her off at Circus Circus, she knew he was divorced, two kids, the older boy in trouble; his lady friend wasn't legal and she just might have a bun in the oven; the best mall was within walking distance; no, he'd never heard of Tammy Diller—nor were people real likely to answer questions in this town—but his cousin Harry would give her a deal at his restaurant. They'd shared so much by that time that Rebecca gave him a hug, as well as his twenty bucks.

Circus Circus, thankfully, had a room. It also seemed to be the only place in town where kids were allowed. Possibly not the best place to find Tammy Diller, but a place with children seemed the least alien of anything Rebecca had noticed so far. A nap, a shower and a change of clothes were her next priorities. The real action, the cabdriver had told her, wouldn't start until sundown. The hustlers and serious gamblers rarely came out of the woodwork before then.

She turned the key on a rose-and-white room, dropped her luggage, sank onto the mattress to test the bed and didn't wake up for the next four hours. The nap refreshed her. She ordered milk and a peanut butter sandwich from room service, then opened her suitcases and turned on the shower.

Time for grooming. On her first studying drive through town, she could see it didn't matter what anyone wore; her teddy-bear sweatshirt would have done fine. But she had in mind seeking out a hustler—namely Ms. Diller—which called for hustler attire.

She hadn't brought any gold lamé. Didn't own any. But, being a Fortune, she could drip a few diamonds if she had to. She washed, dried, spritzed her hair into an abandoned tumble, painted up her eyes with the finest Fortune Cosmetics goop, wrestled into black stockings with seams, splashed on perfume, and then finished her milk and peanut butter sandwich with one eye on her cocktail dress.

The dress was blacker than sin and the closest thing she owned to wicked. She shimmied into it. The crepe was a long-sleeved sheath, respectable enough in front, but with no back. At all. She slipped into crepe high heels, decked all available surfaces with some jewelry glitter, and then she was done—except for a last critical glance in the mirror.

She didn't quite look like a painted-up hussy, but cripes, it was the best she could do.

Two guys tried propositioning her in the elevator, which reassured her that her appearance was up to snuff, but she forgot about them once the elevator opened on the first floor.

Before even trying to look for Tammy, she figured she'd better get a taste of the ambience of the place. So she just wandered for a while. There was excite-

ment, noise, action in every nook and cranny, colors
flashing, lights blurring past with dizzying speed.
Waitresses circulated with free drinks. Slot machines
incessantly clanged and sang out winnings. The
blackjack and roulette tables were a tad more elegant
and subdued, but there was hunger in the air, a hunger to win, the hunger to risk gleaming in strangers'
eyes—and, sometimes, desperation. Studying the
gamblers appealed to her writers' instincts—when
would she ever have another chance to do hands-on
research on such a fascinating aspect of human nature?

Yet, accidentally, she found herself on the second
floor. The thing was, she heard the sound of children
laughing, and just accidentally peeked up there. She
hadn't meant to linger. But it was so different from
all the adult flimflam downstairs. Kids were giggling
and racing everywhere, with live circus acts set up
to entertain them and carnival games all over the
place.

Ten minutes later, she won a stuffed animal, and
gave it to a little blond moppet who'd been crying
over a bumped knee. Since Rebecca was a good aim,
and the word spread that she was giving away her
"wins," she attracted a pint-size audience. The em-
ployee manning the hit-the-duck booth probably
shouldn't have let her play—she was unmistakably
over eighteen—but keeping the kids happy was his
job. He didn't seem to mind bending the rules.

She'd just whirled around to hand a fancy white

unicorn to a ragamuffin little urchin when she noticed the shoes. Loafers. Man-size loafers. Big man-size loafers, followed by a long, long stretch of dress pants... Her eyes zipped past the bulge at his zipper...trailed up a brawny chest in white linen, took in the long arms folded patiently across that huge expanse of chest. She gulped.

Her eyes shot straight to Gabe's, then. Her heart was thumping harder than when she was a kid, scared of finding an alligator under the bed. Gabe was no alligator—in fact, he looked damn near breathtaking in dress clothes, pure vital, virile male, and sexier than was safe for a woman—but there wasn't much question from his expression that he was ticked off.

The kids scattered. If she'd been short enough, she'd have tried to blend in and take off with them. Gabe didn't say anything for a minute, just kept looking her over from head to toe, from the swirl of spritzed curls to the figure-hugging black sheath to her slim legs in seamed stockings. Something kindled in his eyes. Heat. Definitely heat. But it seemed to be motivated a whole lot more by fury than by desire.

"Well, hi, there," she tried cheerfully. "Were you, um, by any chance looking for me?"

"God, no. I knew you'd have the good sense to fly home to Minnesota. I knew you'd listened to reason and understood that it was potentially dangerous—and sure as hell counterproductive—for you to play Nancy Drew any further. I told myself I didn't have to worry about you. I told myself, I know that woman has a brain and surely I can count on her to use it—''

"Now, Gabe, just cool down. If you yell at me in public, cutie, I'll have to punch you in the nose, and that'll upset the children. And I *did* listen to reason. You just don't reason things the same way I do. And you *know* I've already uncovered a number of leads that you weren't able to come up with yourself, so I've surely already proven that I can be of serious, real help—''

Wrong tack to take, she decided. The frown on his forehead deepened into an ominous scowl. The eyes snapped like hot black coals. Perhaps it was best to divert him into thinking about something else. "How on earth did you find me here?"

"That was easy. Most of this town is set up for adults. There's only a few places for someone who's hopelessly addicted to children. If you were anywhere in town, it had to be here. *Where* are your shoes, shorty?''

"Shoes?" She glanced down. Her stockinged toes wiggled back at her. She didn't specifically remember taking off the spike heels, but they sure were killers on her spine. "I, um, don't know. But they have to be around here somewhere—''

"Well, we'll find the shoes, Red. And then you and I are going to have a little talk."

Six

Gabe might want to talk, Rebecca mused, but she noticed he didn't suggest the privacy of either of their hotel rooms to do it in. No way was he risking any clinches *this* night. With some amusement—and fascination—she noted that he was giving her the same wide berth he'd give a loose cougar.

She slipped off her heels—again. No reason not to. She doubted anyone in this town would leap to any judgmental conclusions if she walked around stark naked—except, perhaps, Gabe—and her feet hurt from teetering around on high heels.

There was no shortage of watering holes in and around the casinos, but Gabe had chosen a particularly quiet spot, and led her to a secluded corner table besides. Keno numbers flashed over the bar, but otherwise they were removed from the incessant sparkle and glitter. Rich, dark paneling backdropped red velvet chairs and cushion-soft carpeting. A navy damask tablecloth hid her stockinged feet, and a seductive candle flickered in the middle of the table.

Gabe ordered some kind of strange beer, and rolled his eyes when she asked for a glass of milk. There, now, she thought. His sense of humor was reviving. Truthfully, a snifter of brandy would probably help her sleep better, but the milk would do. Since he hauled her away from the kids, he'd been wearing a scowl. Once the waiter served them and he slugged down a few sips of that strange dark ale, he seemed inclined to be reasonable again.

Perhaps, though, she was being a tad optimistic. Gabe started the conversation by kindly and meticulously laying out all the information he'd picked up on Tammy Diller. Rebecca was astounded that he was suddenly willing to be so helpful and open. At least with her. Gradually, though, she realized the obvious. Slick didn't really *want* her to know anything. He was just spilling enough information to convince her that this Tammy was bad news, and someone a milk drinker should definitely avoid.

Rebecca swung a leg under her, far more interested in the information than in Gabe's newest ploy to get her to go home. "So we know for sure this Tammy's using fake ID—and has before. We know she's traveling with a boyfriend, that she's about thirty-five, not bad-looking. We know she likes hobnobbing with high rollers—judging from her fondness for accumulating credit charges at the best stores and best hotels—and we can pin her down to being in Minneapolis around the time of Monica's death from a hotel charge. Which may not be motive. But it sure shows opportunity, if we could just come up with some direct evidence. We also know she has no record of any job or source of income to be paying for the life-style she seems so fond of living. Have I missed anything so far?"

"Not a thing. That's the general package."

"Dammit, Gabe. We're so close. I know she's Monica's murderer, I can just smell it. And if we could just get a look at her in person, get a chance to talk to her, I just *know* we could find out the link she has to Monica.... What hotel did you say she was staying at, by the way?"

"Don't waste your time flashing those innocent eyes at me, shorty. I didn't say where she was staying, nor am I going to. There's only one reason I filled you in on this—"

"Trust me. I can guess the reason. You wanted to try talking me into staying out of this. Again." She lowered her voice three octaves to imitate Gabe's growly baritone. "The cards aren't all in on Ms. Diller, but she's looking shadier and shadier. And if there's even the remotest chance she was involved in Monica's murder, she isn't likely to appreciate strangers poking questions in her life. It could tick her off. A bad idea, to tick off someone capable of murder. I'd be a lot safer if I'd go home and bake cookies. Oatmeal raisin, chocolate chip, snickerdoodles..."

"Sounds like you've got my whole speech down pat. Except for the cookies. I wouldn't have risked a club over the head for making that kind of sexist remark."

"Hey, you'd have been safe. I love making cookies. In fact, I'll be exuberantly thrilled to go home and do just that...the very instant my brother's out of jail and cleared of this murder charge.'' Her voice turned quiet. She'd given up believing that Gabe could understand her point of view. But she still hoped that he might accept that this was not an issue she could bend on.

Gabe abruptly cleared his throat. ''You could end up in jail yourself if you keep stripping in public.''

She blinked, unsure where the sudden turn in the conversation had come from, and then she chuckled. ''Now, I haven't taken off any clothes but shoes. Yet. But the jewelry was driving me nuts. It's heavy. And all the clasps pick.'' She unhooked her necklace, and laid it on the building pile of spangles on the table— bracelet, ring, and dangling earrings. The only jewelry she'd ever loved wearing was her mom's charm bracelet.

The puddle of jewels flashed fire in the candle-light, and picked up the glint of flame in Gabe's eyes. Stripping off the jewelry, removing her shoes, curling on one leg...Rebecca was suddenly aware that she rarely exhibited ''company behavior'' around Gabe. From the beginning, she'd instinctively trusted him enough to freely be herself around him. His response around her seemed to be the opposite. Poor baby, he was washing a hand over his face again.

''Could you maybe put that stuff in your purse or something? Before you attract every thief and con artist in a ten-mile radius?''

"I didn't bring a purse. And it isn't really the family diamonds, Gabe, just good fakes, but you're welcome to stash it all in your pocket, if you're worried about it."

He promptly scooped the jewels out of sight. "If you don't have a purse, where'd you put your room key?"

"In my shoe." She reached for the glass of milk. "Along with a quarter. I doubt I'll shake that habit even when I'm ninety. The rule was engrained from the time I was four, always to have the money to call home. Tomorrow, I think I'm going to head out to one of those whorehouses."

Her last comment made him choke on a sip of beer. "I beg your pardon?"

"Didn't you see the signs all over town? Prostitution's legal here."

"I *know* prostitution's legal here. But my ears must have been ringing from listening to those slot machines, because I know you didn't say any damn crazy thing about going near one of those places."

"Your hearing's fine, love bug." Gabe seemed to do much better when she didn't give him a chance to think about any one thing for too long. "There's just incredible research potential for a mystery writer here. I've never laid eyes on a compulsive gambler. Or a hustler. And for sure, I've never had an opportunity to see a whorehouse—"

"You're trying to give me a heart attack," he announced.

"Just out of curiosity, have you?"

"Have I had a heart attack?"

"No, silly. Have you ever been to a prostitute?" She waved a hand. "Don't waste your breath telling me you don't have to pay for it. Obviously, I know that. You're adorable, cutie. And you're a grown man, can't imagine what you'd find appealing about a cold-blooded sex act... Do you have a headache?"

Abruptly he stopped rubbing his forehead. "I'm getting one. Trying to follow this conversation could give anyone a migraine. Somehow I didn't expect these questions to come up from a milk drinker. Do you, uh, regularly ask guys you barely know questions about their sex lives?"

Prim as a nun, she raised her eyebrows. "You must have been raised in that school with my dad. He always said that a lady never brought up sex, religion or politics in a conversation—but I'm afraid that lesson went in one ear and out the other with me. I love all three. And I'm a writer. How can I learn anything if I don't talk to people and ask questions? It's my job."

"An accidental excuse to be nosy, you mean."

"That, too." She grinned. "Your job gives you an excuse to be nosy, the same way, so you'd better be careful where you throw stones. And in the meantime, you're evading the question. I know some boys get roped into going to, um, ladies of the night to lose their virginity, a rite of initiation, so to speak—"

"A tick wouldn't be this relentless with a hound. What's it gonna take to get you off this subject?"

"Just an answer," she said demurely.

"Fine. No, I've never been with a hooker, as a 'rite of initiation' or for any other reason."

"Well then, who did you lose your virginity with?"

"A thirty-three-year-old married woman who seduced me when I was fourteen. Now, are you happy you wormed that information out of me?"

"God. A real-life Mrs. Robinson?" Rebecca set down her milk glass with a *thunk.* "That's child abuse."

"That's long-dead history," he corrected her.

"Of course it isn't, Devereax. No one ever forgets their first experience. Whether it's bad or good has a huge effect on whether we're comfortable with the opposite sex, what we think lovemaking is about, what we think relationships are—"

"Ah, Rebecca? I don't know what psychology book you read, but that 'relationship' wasn't worth any heavy analysis. She was hot. She didn't have a moral in sight. She figured a teenage boy'd have stamina. I did. When I found out she was married, I moved along. End of story. I don't suppose you've finished that glass of milk and are ready for bed by now?"

"Pretty soon." His voice reeked of fake desperation—typical of Gabe's dry humor, Rebecca mused. She also noticed he'd loosened his top shirt button and stretched out his long legs. When they first walked in, he'd been wired for sound. No matter how much he believed he was appalled by the conversation, he'd slowly, sneakily relaxed with her. He was having a good time. She wondered if he realized it. "I wasn't just asking you idle questions, you know. The stuff about your Mrs. Robinson and the prostitutes was all relevant to our locating this Tammy Diller."

"I can't *wait* to hear what conceivable logic you used to come to that conclusion," he said wryly.

Rebecca cupped her chin in her palms. On this subject, she couldn't be more serious. "Well... however or whyever Tammy turned out that way, she sounds like a con artist. Someone who lives off her wits, if not her body. Neither ethics nor the law seem high on her worry list. She's into risk. Possibly, earning something honestly doesn't even appeal to her. Scheming's more fun, more challenging. And she's looking for a 'big deal' that'll give her a fast ride on the money gravy train."

Gabe shook his head. "Damned if I know how you could come up with all that from what little I told you, but you get ten brownie points for intuition. That's pretty much how I read her, too, but I still don't know where you're going with this...."

"I'm just trying to figure her out. If she's in town, how are we going to find her? Who's she going to hang out with? I'd guess she'd try to find some kind of rich chicken to pluck, so to speak. And I'm serious about going out to a whorehouse—"

"No," Gabe interjected, "you're not."

"Now, I have no reason to think we'd find her in a place like that, and nothing you told me makes me think she's a prostitute. But I think there's a common denominator in that kind of personality, Gabe. No different than a woman who'd use her body to earn a living, Tammy has a history of using her looks and appearance as bait. And, darn it, that keeps ringing some kind of memory bells for me, but I just can't seem to pin down why...."

"Likely you remember some fictional character you put in some book. Somehow I don't think you've been on hugging terms with too many hustlers in real life, Red."

He loved to get in those licks about her sheltered life. She wasn't about to rise for that sucker hook this time. "The point is that finding Tammy is one problem, but knowing how to handle her is another. I figure if I had a chance to talk to some ladies of the night, I'd have a better understanding of—"

"Rebecca. Read my lips. To begin with, no one's going to let you in the dude ranches. You're female. Not the clientele they're looking for. And secondly, you go near any one of those places and I'll strangle you with my bare hands."

"Gabe?"

"What?"

"I'm pretty sure you have a temper. I'm also

pretty sure you could hold your own in an alley fight. But even if you were mad enough to blow a gasket, you'd never lay a finger on me.'' He didn't seem to like hearing that obvious truth, because he glowered at her with one of his prizewinning intimidating scowls. She grinned...then ducked her head, peered under the tablecloth for her shoes and came up with the heels swinging from one hand. ''One of these days, I'm gonna ask you where that protective streak comes from, cutie. But right now I *have* to go to bed. I'm so beat I can hardly keep my eyes open.''

''We're not finished with this discussion.''

''I know. You want to meet around noon or so tomorrow? The lobby here?''

''Yeah. That'll do.''

She stood up, unable to stop a yawn from escaping. There was a ton of emotion in his dark, shadowed eyes. Frustration—a familiar response that she seemed to evoke in Gabe. Relief—as if trying to deal with her exhausted him, and he was mighty happy she was disappearing to bed. But some other emotion played in his eyes, too.

It was just for an instant that his gaze brushed over her, her tumbled curls by candlelight, her figure in the sleek black sheath, her cream skin catching the glow of flame and shadow. There'd been no desire in his eyes before this. If anything, he'd given her the same respectful distance he'd give a loaded Uzi. But there was desire now...followed rapidly by an expression of alarm, as she rose from the table and leaned over him.

"Night, love bug." He was frozen more solid than an ice cube when she bent down and impulsively brushed her lips over his forehead. The kiss was soft, swift, the contact lighter than the stroke of a feather and over faster than a finger snap. Yet her heart was suddenly racing, racing. Under that ice-cube brow was one hell of a potent fever.

She straightened, avoiding his eyes as if they could bite her, and with deliberate casualness swung her heels over one shoulder. "Try not to worry. We're going to make a great team on this little problem, darlin'."

She escaped before he could say anything. Within five minutes, she had disappeared into the elevator and strode down the hall and was safe and sound behind the locked door of her room.

She tossed her shoes, flopped on the bed and stared blankly at the ceiling. Her brother's face popped into her mind. Jake's. Jake, at fifty-four, was significantly older than she was, and when she last saw him, he'd been behind bars. Jake was so naturally handsome and distinguished—but not in that place. He'd looked gaunt, all his dynamic energy and spirit crippled by being trapped in that horrible cell. Adam, Jake's son, had confided that he did not believe his dad would survive a year if he was convicted.

Rebecca didn't believe he could survive it, either. Gabe thought she was playing with this investigation, she knew. It wasn't so. She joked when she was afraid. That was just her way of coping. The family had long teased her with the tag "the intrepid Rebecca," because she charged into problems head-first, her own way, and no one had ever seen her scared of anything.

She was scared of failing her brother, though.

And she was increasingly afraid of her building, disturbing feelings for Gabe. A simple kiss, no more than a gesture of affection, had her pulse charging like a souped-up jalopy. Always, she'd trusted her instincts. Always, she'd listened to her heart, but even an intrepid optimist of a risk-taker should be able to recognize danger when it slapped her in the face.

Gabe drew her like a storm on a parched summer night. He touched her, and she no longer felt that arid aloneness. When she was with him, even just talking, there was excitement, an electric connection. Way, way beyond any sexual pull, he reminded her of Jake. Lord. Not because her feelings for him were brotherly. But Gabe seemed trapped, not unlike her brother. There were prisons and there were prisons, and Gabe seemed to have put up bars between himself and any hope of love.

Damned stupid to think she could get through those bars, though. Gabe didn't want kisses from her. He'd made that clear as a mirror last time. He was antifamilies, antibabies, and if his rough background was the source of those feelings, that didn't mean that Rebecca had the power to change them—or him.

She felt as lost trying to help her brother as she did trying to understand Gabe. Both, though, could be hurt if she made mistakes. She couldn't afford to fail with her brother.

And she was increasingly afraid that she could lose her heart unless she put a careful lid on her feelings for Gabe.

Gabe paced the lobby, jingling the change in his pocket, then yanked out his hand and looked at his watch again. Three o'clock. Well, 2:56, to be precise. But the four-minute difference was moot.

Gabe never panicked. Give him any crisis, he stayed cool. He'd gotten a couple of medals in the Special Forces, for Pete's sake, because he could keep his head in any situation.

At the moment, enough adrenaline was gushing through his veins for him to spontaneously combust. Where *was* that damn redhead?

He'd never trusted her to make their agreed-upon noon meeting time. Hell, Rebecca could have been up and out and caused a couple of wars before noon. He'd called her room at 9:00 a.m. No answer. He'd redialed at ten, then eleven, paced the familiar carpet in the lobby at noon, left, checked back at one and then two.

Impatiently he slammed out the front doors again, and tried to search the street in both directions. The searing-bright sun made him squint. Taxis hooted, and dozens of passersby cluttered the sidewalks, but there was no sign of a five-foot-five redhead.

He stalked back inside, raked a hand through his hair, then checked his watch again. Two fifty-nine. Three minutes since he'd checked the last time. He was gonna kill her when he caught up with her. If she was hurt or in trouble, he was gonna kill her worse.

The only thing keeping his blood pressure from blowing like a volcano was the sure knowledge that she couldn't have been directly in the path of trouble—because he *had* been. Keeping Rebecca safe was a full-time job, but dammit, he had a *serious* job he was being paid for that needed doing. Rebecca couldn't have located Tammy Diller and the woman's sidekick boyfriend—because Gabe had.

Circus Circus would have been an ideal metaphorical place for those two clowns to stay. But enough digging, and Gabe had scared up the address for the hardscrabble apartment those two had rented outside of town. Once he located the address, he'd driven there, walked around, knocked on doors, talked to neighbors. The two were definitely flopping in that ramshackle shack, but were temporarily not around.

They could wait, now that Gabe had their home base pinned down.

Rebecca couldn't.

She couldn't, he promised himself, have seriously intended to go out to any of those whorehouses. She liked to tease. She called him "cutie" and "love bug" to get his goat, had always taken merciless pleasure in getting a rise out of him.

Rebecca only had to walk in a room to get a rise out of him, and Gabe wasn't thinking in metaphorical terms. The dress she'd worn last night would tempt a monk. Those long legs, that soft cream skin by candlelight, that wild sexy hair, the impish devil in her eyes...she was a test, Gabe decided. Was there a woman alive who could drive him insane? Obliterate the control he'd counted on his entire adult life?

He glared at every stranger in the lobby, shoveled a hand through his hair again, and then stomped over to the house phones. He'd call her room one more time. If she didn't answer this time, he didn't know what he was going to do. Start calling hospitals, police, the marines—or her mother—and since none of them were likely to be able to control the damn woman...

He'd just picked up the house phone when he saw a blur of color racing past.

He recognized the fanny first. There weren't many women running around with that one. Just her, and blindfolded in a back alley, Gabe would know that minuscule bouncing tush. He hung up the phone. The fear clawing in his pulse slowly, slowly simmered down. She wasn't hurt. She wasn't in trouble.

She was ramming around the lobby so fast that it'd have been easier to halt a speeding bullet. Still, he caught sight of the oversize Mickey Mouse T, the scraped-into tight jeans, the tennies with the fluorescent green laces and the chunk of gold flashing on her wrists. Her hair was a fuzzfest of curls, no goop on it today. Flashing around this fast, if he hadn't known her, he might have mistaken her for a twelve-year-old.

He not only knew her. He'd touched her. She was more full-blown woman trouble than Lorelei had been for the sailors in that old tale. No telling why she was dressed so ditsy, but she was definitely a stinging shot of life in a lobby that'd seemed damn pale until she raced through. Relief chugged through his bloodstream, singing rich.

Thank God she was alive…so he could kill her.

"*Gabe!*" Finally she spotted him. Zigzagging through bodies and travelers' suitcases, she galloped toward him. Her enthusiastic grin was bigger than sunshine. "Guess what!"

She didn't seem to have the first clue that he intended—could hardly *wait*—to mop the floor with her. The damn fool redhead was so excited she hurled her arms around his neck.

Seven

"**Y**ou're late." Gabe certainly meant to yell the admonishment, but something happened to his voice. For that instant when her arms were looped around his neck, she was impossibly close. Her hair smelled like fresh strawberries, her lips were parted and her skin was baby-soft, and suddenly his throat went bone-dry.

He knew she meant nothing more than an affectionate gesture, an exuberant impulse. Both were typical of her. Rebecca never curbed the expressing of emotion. She freely trusted too damn much in life—doubtless because of her moneyed, sheltered background—yet that hug somehow pulled at him, yanked his personal chain more than the hottest-spiced kiss. He wasn't used to affection. Didn't expect it, didn't ask for it, from anyone. And damnation, he'd never figured he'd ever missed something as foolish and stupid and inconsequential as affection. Until her.

"I know I'm late. And I'm real sorry. I couldn't help it." Her eyes met his for a heartbeat—no more, not even a second more. Slowly her arms slid away from his neck, dropped, and suddenly she was bubbling with more chitchat than a magpie. "I was in one of the back-room poker games, Gabe. Big money back there, whew, a real cutthroat crowd, but it wasn't that easy to suddenly pick up and leave. I knew how late it was getting, but it's considered bad manners to take off when you're winning. I could have fixed that by throwing a few hands. But the thing was, I was learning so many things—''

"You were in one of those back-room high-stakes poker games?" he asked again, because it was possible he'd misheard. He hoped he'd misheard.

"Yup. In fact, that's why I wore my Mickey Mouse T." She motioned to the big ears on her chest with a grin. "I figured the guys would peg me for a sucker, you know? More to the point, someone they didn't have to worry about trusting or talking to. Anyway…guess what?! I'd hoped Tammy might have been hanging around one of those high-roller games, and she *has* been, Gabe! One of the guys knew her, told me all kinds of things about her—and about her boyfriend, too. Boy, I'm having a low-blood-sugar attack—you think there's anyplace in this town we could get an ice cream cone?"

She didn't really want ice cream. She wanted the healthier, fancier frozen yogurt, preferably raspberry-flavored. It took a bit to track that down. Then, because she was sick of sitting still, she chose to eat it walking. It was blistering-hot outside, the sun blinding-bright, and the yogurt was trying to dribble and melt on her from every direction. She zigzagged around pedestrians, her tongue lapping at that raspberry cone, her eyes dancing with all her news.

"Tammy's been hanging out at Caesar's Palace, also a place called O'Henry's—especially this O'Henry's place. I'm not talking about the two-dollar tables out front, but the big-money action in the back rooms. And, Gabe... I really don't believe this—the guy was probably just talking—but he made out like he'd slept with her."

"Uh, shorty, I don't think Tammy ever read a real long rule book on morals." He grabbed another napkin from his pocket. She lifted her chin so he could take a swipe. Damn good thing he'd brought a handful of napkins.

"You don't understand. She was with her boyfriend. *And* this guy. I mean...both of them. At least that's sure as heck what he was implying."

Perhaps, Gabe thought, his fascination with her was logically understandable. He'd never met a woman who wore diamonds and drank milk. Or discussed sexual threesomes in between licks on an ice cream cone. "How," he said carefully, "did this totally strange man start talking about his sex life with you?"

"He didn't *start* talking about sex. We were playing five-card draw, for heavens sake. Eventually I got around to saying that I was looking for an old school friend whose name was Tammy Diller...and right off, this guy's eyes lit up, and suddenly he was winking and posturing at the other men around the table,

telling this story. He didn't actually *say* the words—
it was all in disgusting little innuendos. He was a
real jerk, Gabe. Like I said, I don't necessarily believe that part of what he said—but he also described
her. Dark brown hair, brown eyes, medium to tallish,
slender... I almost laughed—she sounds like half the
women in my family. Only he was mostly going on
about certain embarrassing physical features besides
that. Holy smokes, she just met him! And I can't
believe any woman would—''

Gabe had a bad feeling that she was willing to
dwell on that threesome scene indefinitely. Worse
yet, she appeared more than willing to share every
embellishing detail with him. Driven to shift her
mind to a different track, he interrupted with the information he'd learned about the twosome—from the
name of Tammy's boyfriend, Dwayne, to the location of their rented digs and where Ms. Diller was
clocking up credit-card charges.

The information diverted Rebecca's mind from
sex. But it didn't exactly save him from her pursuit
of more troublesome subjects. "Damn. I could swear
I've heard that Dwayne's name before. Something
keeps itching in the back of my mind. Somehow I
think I know this woman some way—''

"Ah. Is this your infamous women's intuition at
work again?''

She finished the cone, and licked her fingers with
a giant grin. "You keep making fun of my intuition,
you skeptic, but it isn't just your logic that's gotten

us this far. Didn't I tell you it'd work out this way? We got double the information, by coming at this from two entirely different angles. Ask me, we make a pretty unbeatable team. And what do you think? Should we check out this O'Henry's place tonight?''

Gabe heard her test out that ''we make a good team'' philosophy the night before. If she hadn't skipped out before giving him a chance, she'd have heard his ''over my dead body'' philosophy. Now, though, he hesitated.

It was pretty tough to deny—even if it grated—that Rebecca was pulling her weight in this investigation so far. Of course, it was luck that she'd found the Tammy/Monica letter. And luck that she'd chanced on a man who knew Tammy. She was intuitive and perceptive, Gabe was willing to concede, but working as a team was out of the question. He worked alone. Always had. It was faster, safer, more efficient. And by his sense of honor and values, there was no way he could justify allowing Rebecca anywhere near a dangerous situation.

Unfortunately, he was coming to the painful and annoying conclusion that Ms. Rebecca Idealist Fortune was a menace on her own. She'd nearly killed herself breaking into Monica's house. She'd blindly taken off cross-country—twice now—without a thought about consequences. And the kind of company she started chance conversations with—that gang-size bruiser in L.A., the cretin bragging about threesomes that she'd found in that back-room poker game—was enough to give Gabe a case of hives. He'd never been prone to hives.

He'd never met a woman who was kissing kin to an adult Dennis the Menace before, either.

"Gabe, did you hear me? Don't you think it'd be a good idea for us to go to O'Henry's tonight?" she questioned again.

Obviously, she was too antsy for an answer to give him five seconds to think it through. Thinking probably wouldn't help this problem, anyway. There were no *good* answers regarding Rebecca—except that she was safer in his sight than out of it. "Fine with me," he said curtly. "We'll hit Caesar's. We'll hit O'Henry's. We'll make the run of all the places traditionally associated with big money. I want some ground rules agreed on first, though, shorty."

"Sure."

"You stick with me. No wandering off on your own."

"Okay," Rebecca agreed.

"Our goal is to locate her. See the lay of the land she's trying to map out here. Then we'll decide how to approach her, not before."

"Makes good sense," Rebecca agreed.

"And assuming we find her—I don't want her knowing you're a Fortune. I don't want her knowing you have any association with Jake—or Monica. You stay quiet as a mouse, no starting a conversation with her or any other strangers. And if we do find her, that's it—you're out of here."

She turned to him with a frown. He braced for an argument. His pulse bucked for an entirely different reason when she lifted a hand and, like it was her business, straightened the collar of his shirt. "You really have to stop worrying about me," she said gently. "I've been on my own a long time. I can take care of myself, Gabe."

The hell she could. Gabe guessed any comment he made would come out sexist and earn him a feminist tongue-lashing. But it wasn't her strength as a woman that he doubted, or, in spite of his teasing, her brain. Rebecca was no ditz, but, tarnation, the woman believed in love. She believed in white knights, that right would prevail, that nothing would hurt her. Since she'd been protected by the Fortune empire her whole life, he didn't blame her for such innocence. She'd just never been exposed to the rougher side of life.

But her idealism made her vulnerable.

The strange thought crossed his mind that he didn't want to change her. He wanted her to stay free, to believe in all that impossibly wholesome "good," to stay exactly who she was. But it sure made protecting her difficult.

A knife twisted in his gut at the thought of anything happening to her. A sharp, serrated knife, with a painfully pointed blade.

Until that moment, he'd assumed any wayward feelings he had for Rebecca were hormone-caused.

They'd better be.

If there was a woman on earth he had no business seriously caring about, it was her.

"Well, blast and damnation. I feel like kicking a wall, throwing some priceless china, punching somebody's nose—"

"Far be it from me to interrupt a lady's tantrum, but do you think you could pause just long enough to come up with your room key?"

Ignoring the irrepressible humor in his eyes, Rebecca clapped her hotel room key into his palm. "I'm *frustrated,* Devereax."

"No kidding?"

"Oh, come in and have a drink with me and quit being so damned annoying. I swear, you'd stay cool in a riot. Don't you ever lose it? Let down your hair and just have yourself a good old-fashioned scream-or cryfest?"

"Uh...no." Gabe's tone was dry. And from the time they arrived back at the hotel, he'd been in gentlemanly take-charge mode, as far as walking her up to her room and unlocking the door, but now he cleared his throat at her invitation to come in. "It's way past midnight now. Pretty late, as far as a drink—"

"Don't tell me you're ready to sleep. You're as wired as I am. And not to panic—I wasn't going to offer to serve you milk. I travel with a flask. Can't remember whether I put Scotch or whiskey or what in it, but I can promise you something more lethal than lactose.''

Something still made him hesitate, but hell's bells, he'd already stepped past the threshold to pull the key from the lock. Rebecca closed the door and motioned him toward the table and chairs crowded in one corner, and after that he had the sense to stay out of her way.

She kicked off her heels, hurled her purse on the bed, fetched two glasses from the bathroom and then buried her head in her suitcase. Out came the flask. Then a hefty package of Gummi Bears, a tin of trail mix, and a serious two-pounder of M&M's. All the items soared through the air, helter-skelter, toward Gabe.

He caught the goodies, but she caught the rumble of a chuckle as he settled back in the corner chair, stretching out his long legs. "You, uh, always pack a private food stash?"

"Always. A woman needs real sustenance from time to time. Living off restaurant meals just doesn't cut it.... *Dammit,* we were barely a step behind those jokers every place we went. If our timing had been five seconds better, we could have touched them. For Pete's sake, it had to be a miracle we *didn't* run into them.''

"At least we know for sure they're here. And that they're in no sense trying to hide, but operating out in the open and visible.''

"But to be so close and keep missing them... How come you're not as aggravated as I am, you cretin?"

"Because I think it's best Ms. Diller doesn't lay eyes on you, shorty. We learned a ton tonight. More than enough to make some results possible, and even likely, tomorrow."

Well, they *had* learned quite a bit. Rebecca threw herself in the opposite chair and slouched in it, low, cocking her stockinged feet on the bed and crossing her ankles. Did no good. She could make herself sit still, but she couldn't stop her mind from spinning a hundred miles an hour. Glittery jewelry popped out of Gabe's pocket—the jewels he'd forgotten to return from the night before. She'd forgotten them, too.

She glanced down, thinking the little black number she was wearing could have used some fancying-up. Earlier, Gabe had taken one glance and had a minor heart attack at her showing up in the lobby in nothing more than a slip.

It wasn't, of course, a slip. It was a perfectly respectable ridiculously expensive spaghetti-strapped scrap of material that reached all the way to midthigh. No bra possible, but beggars couldn't be choosers. She'd only had a few minutes to chase into a boutique that afternoon—who'd have guessed she'd need so many dressy clothes for this impromptu trip? She was lucky to find something that fit her.

Her talisman charm bracelet jangled as she spilled out some M&M's, and automatically started sorting them by color. Tammy Diller, from what they'd heard, had been running around braless, too. And had quite a reputation for color. Red dress. Slits front and back. Flaunting everything that was legal and a few views that weren't—for the right men—her whole program delivered with a New Orleans drawl, a mouth painted scarlet, and sultry-styled dirty blond hair.

Sounded like a female eel to Rebecca. And Tammy's sidekick, this Dwayne fellow, had been decked out in a tux, a skinny blond man with a boyish charm—especially when sidling up to plump dowagers. The two jokers had been dressed like they had it to burn, and were pushing a big-talk real estate scheme on anyone who'd listen.

They had enough funds to get in some serious blackjack games, but they didn't play long anywhere. Both were too smart to gamble their capital. That was just their advertising budget. But those damn two had been at every single place she and Gabe stopped. Every place. Only every damn time, Tammy and Dwayne-boy seemed to have just left.

"You didn't do real good at sticking by my side," Gabe mentioned.

"Well, of course I didn't. It would never have done any good for the two of us to be connected with an umbilical cord. Strangers were always going to tell you entirely different things than they'd tell me." She scooped up a handful of the green M&M's—before Gabe could. "I thought that one blonde at Caesar's was gonna trip you right on the floor. You showed remarkable restraint, Devereax. She was adorable."

But no one, Rebecca mused, had been half as adorable as Gabe, anywhere they went. He dominated every room they walked into. He'd shaken off his tux jacket, loosened the top buttons of the pleated linen shirt, and his chin had a pirate's shadow of whiskers now. Didn't matter. The virgin white shirt fabric was still striking against his ruddy skin, his long lean frame a shout of virility in or out of elegant clothes, and those deep, dark, broody eyes had enough devil in them to make any woman edgy. Good-edgy. Wicked-edgy.

Those dark eyes happened to be riveted on her now. "You finally starting to calm down a little?"

"Just because it's two in the morning? Cripes, no." She rubbed two fingers on her temples. "I *need* to help my brother, Gabe. His trial date's coming faster than a tornado now. Finding answers in July won't help worth bananas. I need them *now*. I want him *out* of that place, and his name cleared."

"Now just take it easy and listen." Gabe unscrewed the flask, sniffed it, poured about three inches in her water glass and an inch in his own. "I have staff in the office, working on leads, following through on a dozen other sources of information. Other facts could turn up at any time to help your brother. Your mother gave me another name to follow up on, in fact, and God knows Monica collected plenty of enemies in her lifetime. I only took on Tammy myself because right now she looked like our best bet. We don't have to *know* if she killed Monica, shorty, and we sure don't have to prove it. All we need is evidence pointing to her as a second viable suspect. If we can connect Tammy to a problem with Monica around the time of the murder—any connection that looks like a motive—it should raise reasonable doubt in a jury's mind, and be enough to get your brother off.''

"Well, that's not enough. Not for me. He didn't *do* it, Gabe. I want who *did* do it hung up by a big, fat rope. My brother needs to be able to hold his head up. And I hate feeling so helpless to do anything that matters for him!''

"Rebecca, you *are* helping him.'' His voice turned low, quiet. "We learned everything we needed to know about that pair tonight. Getting a firsthand look at them would have been nice, but it couldn't matter less. Our goal was discovering what they were up to, and we did that. Knowing about that real estate scheme gave me the information I needed to plan how to approach them, what it'll take to get a conversation going. So no more misjudging how much progress was made tonight.''

She took a sip of the Scotch, an *ugh* taste if ever there was one, yet it shimmered on her tongue, warmed going down her throat. The frazzled nerves were seeping away. So was the exasperation. Her anxiety and need to help her brother hadn't diminished...but somehow being with Gabe put it in perspective. Gabe might not believe in her brother's innocence, but no paltry tornado or earthquake would ever stop him from doing his job. He was thorough, relentless and, thank God, stubborn as a goat.

"You know what?" she murmured. "We really did work well together tonight."

"Yeah." He agreed—but she could see the sudden guarded look in his eyes. Obviously in a hustle to change the subject, he glanced around the hotel room, taking in the rose-print bedspread, the token print over the bed, the cramped walk area. "You didn't land a bad room, but somehow I'd guess wherever you live is real different."

"I'll say." Since he seemed in a mood to listen, she spilled out a haphazard description of her place. "My office is a mess of books, towering and toppling in every direction. I've got an Abe Lincoln teddy bear stashed next to my word processor. I always did love Abe...he failed at everything he tried, but nothing kept him from picking himself up and trying again. I dipped into Mom's attic for most of the furniture—antiques and stuff no one else had a place for. Nothing matches worth beans. I love it, anyway. You'd have a stroke at the bathroom—having an obvious 'in' with the Fortune family, I get first dibs on every cosmetic or scent we're trying out. I'd bet the bank you'd find the whole place a disgusting female lair, probably drive you crazy with all the clutter," she said wryly. "Although I've got a spare bedroom that'd make one beauty of a nursery one of these days."

He avoided the subject of babies as if it were a catchable disease. "Somehow I'd have thought your mother would have pressed to have you live at home."

Rebecca shook her head. "Mom knew better than that. We both did. Pretty hard for two adult women to get along under the same roof. She pushed me about security, but I grew up knowing how important that was. Whether I was directly part of the business or not, having the Fortune name was always going to follow me. But as far as independence...I loved both my parents, and after my dad died, my mom and I became even closer. Still, I have my own work, my own life. Can't imagine still living at home at my age. But how about you? What's your place like?"

"Just an apartment. Four walls. All the appliances that make life easier, but decorating stuff—no. I'm working most of the time, anyway. In fact, I bought a couch-bed to set up in the office about four years ago. Easier to crash there some nights than drive all the way home."

He was just making conversation, but Rebecca could mentally picture the place he described. It sounded spare and impersonal and cold. Not a haven of comfort that a man couldn't wait to come home to after a long day, but lonely. Like him, she thought.

"You know," she said slowly, teasingly, "when I first met you, I thought you were an overbearing, domineering, hopelessly chauvinistic pig. But that's not at all true.''

"Uh…thanks. I think.''

"You take charge,'' she continued softly, "but you're not really bossy. None of that disgusting stuff even shows up unless you're worried about someone. Basically it's just protectiveness.''

"Is this character analysis gonna go on long?''

She smiled. "No. But I'm wondering where that protective streak comes from.''

"Who knows? Who cares?''

"Hey, if you humor me and answer the question, I'll quit bugging you.''

"Don't try to sell *me* swampland, shorty. You're gonna be nosy until you die.'' Maybe he wasn't going to bite at the bribe she'd offered him, yet his gaze rested on her face for a long moment, as if he were considering through whether it was a good idea to answer her straight. "Maybe I do have a bone about being protective. I grew up feeling helpless. My parents fought all the time, and nothing I did or said could make that better. Kids got killed in the street, grade-school cronies got suckered into dope, knife fights, gangs. I couldn't change anybody I cared about. I couldn't protect anybody I cared about then, either.''

Rebecca heard what he said. But she also heard the unspoken message behind the words. The only time Gabe opened up with her was when the information had a purpose—such as meticulously, carefully telling her again that he wasn't for her and they came from entirely different worlds. "So...was that feeling helpless thing part of the reason you decided to join the military?"

"The military was my ticket out of hell. The Special Forces was an even better ticket. I not only learned how to protect the men under me—I had the chance to do it. Responsibility, duty, honor—they all count there. That didn't get old for me, but I did. The Special Forces requires a young man's reflexes and stamina. Investigative work was a pretty natural thing to follow through with when I got out."

"Rules, order, facts. Things you have control over. Things you can make a difference with," she mused.

"I don't think you're exactly fond of taking the predictable road, Red. My choosing 'rules' has to sound pretty dull to you."

"Actually, that sounds like a natural choice for a man who started out frustrated by wrongs and problems he had no possible control over. I never had it rough like that, Gabe." It was the most he'd openly shared about himself, yet Rebecca again suspected that his comments weren't precisely voluntary. His eyes had skidded down her legs, darted away from the dip in her bodice, and much more tellingly, skated away fast from any expression of caring in her face. She never doubted that Gabe was telling the truth about his background. He was a pure-blooded honest man. She just sensed another truth—whenever she expressed the teensiest sign that she cared about him, Sir Gabe Devereax most protectively warned her off by reminding her of the vast differences between them.

She knew their differences. She also knew that falling for a man who didn't believe in babies and families could only end in heartache for her. Yet the risks seemed to have no power over her emotions. She couldn't stop the rain. She couldn't hold a rainbow in her palm.

She could not seem to stop falling hard and deeply, for Gabe.

"Everyone has different crosses to bear," Gabe said. "My version of growing up rough was just different than yours. It couldn't have been easy growing up in the Fortune clan."

"Being part of the Fortune dynasty had some unique challenges. But I was always loved. I always knew it."

"Yeah, well, a lot of people use that word *love*. Cheaper currency than money sometimes," Gabe said drily.

Any other time, she'd have bitten faster than trout for a dangling worm. He'd always teased, played the cynic to her idealist. Both of them enjoyed the wrangling. Rebecca had never minded it. She just suddenly wondered what it would take to get him to move past it.

"Don't," he ordered swiftly.

His stress level certainly seemed to have come from nowhere. All she'd done was lower her feet to the ground and stand up. From the alarm in his eyes, you'd have thought she'd stripped naked in a public casino.

"We both needed a drink to wire down. But now it's time for me to hit the road and find my own room."

"Probably a good idea," she agreed. But she noticed he didn't stop her when she followed through with an entirely different good idea and angled a seat on his lap.

"This is *not* wise, shorty."

"I know."

"We've been doing just fine."

"I know."

"You just ignore chemistry, sooner or later it goes away. No way to get in trouble if you just stay out of its way."

"That's a good theory, but I'm afraid it doesn't always work, Gabe. I think this chemistry's simmering like a pot roast every time we're together. At least it is for me. I can smell the spices. The heat's right there. I don't understand it. How come I feel these things with you? How come I haven't felt them before? What is it with you and me? Questions or problems I don't understand just drive me nuts. Call it a character flaw, but I just can't rest until I have some answers."

"That's a hell of a half-baked reason for sitting on my lap."

"So kick me off," she suggested.

But he didn't.

Eight

He reached for her. Suddenly, roughly. The image sprang into her mind of a shipwrecked sailor yanking hold of a life buoy, the only thing saving him from a dark, wild storm. One of his arms was trapped behind her back, but the other was definitely free.

Tense, callused fingers dived into her hair and buried there, holding her still, holding her quiet, when everything in Rebecca had suddenly gone still and quiet and she most certainly wasn't trying to move away. His mouth crushed on hers with blistering heat and galvanizing pressure.

He tasted…fierce. Like an explosion of loneliness. Like needs trapped so long that the lid was blowing clear off. It was the wildest kiss she'd ever invited, definitely the most dangerous, and her pulse was suddenly charging, charging. Only a dimwit swam in quicksand. She knew Gabe valued control; she knew he'd been a good guy on his terms by keeping his hands off her. He hadn't asked for this. And maybe she was a dimwit for pushing him.

Yet nothing had ever felt so right. All the logical reasons this was wrong and risky and crazy seemed to utterly unimpress her heart.

One kiss, still smoking, became a firestarter for another. His tongue found hers. Took hers. White noise filled her mind; nothing else worth noting existed in the universe at that moment but Gabe. Not for her. No other man had ever been this right. Not for her.

His hand slipped down, seared a path down her long white throat, skated to her shoulder, pushing down the spaghetti strap of her dress at the same time. Her head reeled back. His mouth burned the same path down her throat, kisses involving teeth and a dangerously wet, warm tongue. The kisses sweeping wet fire down her collarbone were bad enough, but her one breast was bared when he pushed down that strap. Bared. And vulnerable.

Gabe was a good man. Beyond their differences, beyond the insurmountable obstacles, beyond any other damn fool silly thing, Rebecca's heart had intuited a long time ago that he was not only a good man, but maybe the best man she'd ever known. Right then, though, he really didn't seem to be highly motivated to be good.

Whiskers tickled the swell of her breast. His mouth discovered the swell, then explored until he found the nipple. He buffed it, polished it shiny with his tongue until the tip wrinkled and tightened. Her breath started coming in loose stitches. Her pulse was rushing like a jet revving for takeoff. Anyway, anyhow, she twisted on his lap, she could feel his arousal growing, pulsing, a clear warning if there ever was one to slow down, cool down and think.

She didn't want to cool down. She'd felt longing before, but not this ache of belonging. She'd felt need before, but not this fever of desire. Her hands pushed at his shirt, past starched linen to fever-warm skin and bristly tufts of chest hair. His skin smelled warm, clean, male. His heart thundered under her touch, his response so real and raw, so honest. Like Gabe. So volatile, like Gabe.

Like a man imprisoned too long in solitary confinement, he seemed to be starving for sunlight. Flavors and textures assaulted her senses. They all seemed to have his name. They all seemed to spell out need. His need, to touch, to connect, to really believe there was another human being on the other side of that lonely, dark abyss. The fierce darkness in his eyes, the sounds he made, the way he kneaded and stroked any skin he could touch…Gabe made her feel like she was his sunlight. Like she was the only one with a key to that prison-cell door for him. Like he needed *her*.

Her response was as natural as rain. She'd never felt this way with another man. Nor did she want to. No different from Gabe, she'd never exposed this vulnerable, naked level of need with anyone else. But with him, she could be honest.

Perhaps too exuberantly honest. She almost poked his eye out, trying to yank his head down for another mouth to mouth kiss. Neither her elbows nor her knees seemed to be in the right place, not to touch him the way she wanted to. She caught a glint of laughter in Gabe's eyes, but there was tension and frustrated desire in his gaze, too.

His breath was coming as fast and rough as her own. She'd curled up her legs—the closest she could come to wrapping around him in that damned annoying chair—and his hand started stroking, a long, slow stroke of caress up the length of her leg. His palm slid against the silk stocking from her calf to her thigh, invoking shivers in his wake, a feeling as if she were sinking, sinking down a velvet intimate well. He pushed up her dress and cupped the curve of her hip, making a gruff aching sound, his voice rough as rust, as much wonder in that sound as there was frustration and raw need.

"Becca..." he whispered fiercely.

And then the telephone rang. The jangling, jingling *brring* startled them both.

Rebecca stared blindly at Gabe for a millisecond, trying to scoop her mind back together. It took several seconds before reality registered—that she was in a hotel room, that the hotel room obviously had a phone, and that the location of said phone was a torturously long distance across the bed.

The phone jangled again, even as Gabe was scooching her off his lap and forcibly standing her up. "Any other time, I'd suggest ripping the phone out from the wall, shorty. But I'm afraid a phone call in the middle of the night like this could well mean something serious. You'd better get it.''

That logic was getting around to occuring to her, just a lot slower than it hit Gabe. She tripped and skittered around the bed to reach the bedside table before the phone could caterwaul another time. "Hello?"

"Rebecca Fortune?"

"Yes, this is Rebecca." She didn't recognize the woman's voice, but then, she might not have recognized her own mother's at that moment. Her whole body was still tuned in to Gabe, singing the blues, humming awareness and drumming low and wild about how close they'd come—how close they were—to making love. She just couldn't concentrate on anything else.

"This is Tammy. Tammy Diller."

If she'd needed a bullet to obliterate desire and force her ability to concentrate, the name announced by her caller worked better than buckshot. With a gulp of a breath, Rebecca sank onto the bed.

"No," Gabe said firmly. "No, no, no. You're not meeting with that woman, Rebecca. Forget it. It's out of the question."

"Now you're just gonna have to calm down, Devereax. I'm not thrilled at the idea, either, but it's not like I have another choice. I have to do this. That's that.''

"That's *not* that, and you're going anywhere near Ms. Diller over my dead body."

"I don't know how Tammy found me—"

"I sure as hell do. You've been asking questions all over town. All over two towns, for that matter. Dangerous questions, about a woman who could damn well be a murderess. Did I yell at you about not doing that? Did I? Dammit, that she managed to track down your name and where you're staying is enough to give me ulcers. You're getting out of sight and going home, shorty. And that isn't a suggestion this time. I mean it."

"You might as well quit yelling. I'm not going anywhere."

"Oh, yeah, you are."

"Gabe, I realize you're worried. So am I. But this is the first serious and real chance I've had to help my brother. Trust me, cutie. There is no one and nothing that's going to stop me."

She said the last in a gentle, quiet, sure voice that made him want to wring her neck.

Since her hotel room was cramped for space, he'd started pacing on one side of the bed. She'd started pacing on the other. Their eyes met on every pivot.

He'd never fought with a woman. Ever. He certainly had never screamed on a vulnerable woman's head. It went against every ethic and instinct about how a man behaved and treated a woman.

Guilt sheared through his conscience in choppy slices. The guilt over yelling at her wasn't too bad—

hell, she was being as bullheaded and stubborn as a hound. If he *had* to wring her idealistic neck to keep her alive and safe, then that was the way the cookie crumbled. He'd intimidated men under his command with half this effort. So far, nothing had intimidated or scared that damned redhead—which struck Gabe as another proof that she was foolhardy and reckless. She *had* no concept of danger.

So far, trying to intimidate her hadn't worked worth beans—but he wasn't through with her yet. He could live with having to be mean to her. In this case, the end sure as hell justified the means.

But there was another brand of guilt slicing at his conscience. Guilt aroused from nothing more than looking at her, and it was the kind of guilt that slapped him like a storm, with dark winds and sharp, piercing spears of lightning.

One of the skinny straps had broken on her dress. The bodice was hanging on the swell of her right breast, threatening further exposure every time she took a breath. Her mouth was scarlet from the pressure of his kisses. Her skin was still soft and flushed from desire.

The glaring overhead light starkly illuminated everything about her. Her hair was like a sunset, shimmering golds and reds in a tangle of light every time she spun around.

The bed between them was a knife-sharp reminder of how close they'd come to tumbling onto it. How much he still wanted to. How much he still wanted her.

There was nothing wrong with wanting a woman. Nothing wrong with sleeping with a willing woman. But, dammit, this was Rebecca. She wanted babies. A family. She didn't have a single life goal that wasn't wholesome.

Gabe couldn't remake himself into a "wholesome" man. Getting naked with a woman was entirely different from getting intimate. He'd never deliberately hurt a woman, never come on to one who didn't play for the same stakes he did.

He'd never let a woman—or anything else—interfere with his work before, either.

"I don't believe I let this go so far," he muttered darkly. "Tammy shouldn't have a clue who you are, Red."

"If she hadn't figured out who I was, she'd never have contacted me," Rebecca said reasonably. "There wasn't anything dangerous in the conversation, for heaven's sakes. Actually, she sounded... nice. She apologized for calling so late. And all she really said was that she'd heard from some friends that I'd been trying to look her up—she didn't know why, but if I wanted to meet, it was okay by her, and she had some free time tomorrow."

Gabe rolled his eyes at her, mimicking a soprano voice. "You should never have bought in, shorty."

"I couldn't wait to 'buy in,' as you put it. We

want to talk to this woman, for Pete's sake. She was dropping the opportunity right in my lap.''

"Yeah. And she miraculously suggested a nice, quiet meeting place in the Red Rock Canyon area to do it. Tammy, Ms. Pollyanna, is no nature spirit. If she picked a deserted location like that, it sure as hell isn't because she wants to meditate with you."

"You're leaping to conclusions," Rebecca said firmly. "We don't *know* that she has anything dangerous in mind. There's no way of knowing anything that's on her mind unless I do this."

"Then we'll never know—because there isn't a prayer of your meeting with that woman alone."

"Gabe, she asked for me. Not you. Now, just stop thinking like an overprotective gorilla for a minute, and think about this. I *have* to go alone. I want to. A woman can always find a way to talk with another woman. She's already volunteered to do this, and whatever she does or doesn't say, I could read her face between the lines. You'd totally mess that up, love bug. Not that you aren't adorable, but you do have a teensy tendency to be intimidating, and you're really lousy at being subtle."

"I'm talking *safety*. I don't give a rat's ass about subtlety."

She had the outright nerve to shoot him a mischievous grin. "I rest my case."

"Rebecca, I don't *like* this."

"I know."

"I don't like *anything* about this."

"I know."

In the end, he gave in—partly, and certainly not willingly. If it had been a choice, he'd have called her mama and had Kate lock her in a convent. As powerful a businesswoman as Kate Fortune was, though, Gabe no longer trusted that she had any power over her daughter. Nobody seemed to have any power over Rebecca—the woman was an ace-pro ulcer-producing walking nightmare.

Unfortunately, she was *his* nightmare. There was no possible way to trust her on her own. Rebecca had a history of slipping the noose when it came to rules. He could put her on a plane, but he couldn't guarantee she wouldn't hijack it and somehow manage to make that meeting with Ms. Diller. He had a nasty feeling that even roped, tied and quartered, Rebecca would still find some way to make that meeting.

So. He set ground rules. She'd go—but he would travel to the location first, in a separate car. She wouldn't see him, but he'd be there. She was to listen, to follow up whatever Tammy volunteered in conversation, but no way, no how, was she to mention Monica's murder. She could make up any fairy tale she wanted to satisfy Tammy's curiosity about why she was asking questions, but she was to duck any dangerous topics.

Rebecca agreed to all those terms without a single hesitation. Gabe didn't mention that he planned to go there armed...or that he would decide whether to stay out of sight, depending on how the whole scene looked and felt when he got there. She didn't ask.

She did, suddenly, yawn. A big, growly, noisy yawn, followed by a big-eyed blink and then a grin. "Fighting with you is sure tiring," she said drily. "Good grief! Do you have any idea what time it is?"

Actually he didn't, but when Gabe glanced at his watch, he immediately reached for his tux jacket. "We'll go all over this again tomorrow, before you go. If you're supposed to meet her at two, let's plan for an early lunch—like eleven. I'll pick you up in your room here."

"That may be lunch for you, but it'll probably be my breakfast. I'm guessing I could easily sleep in that long."

"Good idea," Gabe said. Personally, though, he didn't expect to sleep at all. There were arrangements to be made before tomorrow, from renting a second car to checking out that Red Rock Canyon site ahead of time. He made fast tracks for the door, then abruptly stopped. "Shorty..."

He really wasn't sure what to say, only that something needed saying. The telephone call from Tammy had broken the mood between them as effectively as a swim in the Arctic Ocean. Still, memories of that intimacy were between them now, and could fester into the wrong kind of sore if they didn't deal with them.

Her voice was softer than butter. "Are you planning to apologize for almost making love?"

"Not...apologize." He scrubbed a hand over his face. "Yeah. I want to apologize."

"It seemed to me that I came on to you. Not the other way around." She rubbed a hand over her face, as if the gesture were catching. "I should have my mind on my brother, Gabe. He's the reason I'm here. My head wasn't on straight when Tammy called, and I can't seem to stop feeling guilty about that."

"Well, deguilt, then, Red. Your brother is my job. However much love and loyalty is motivating you...you're not used to this. You're not used to dealing with scum, not used to hightailing it around the country, not used to people who live in shadows." He jammed his hands in his pockets. "You're also worried about your brother. Everything about the situation makes for heightened emotions and unpredictable feelings. When adrenaline's pumping, no one thinks like they normally do."

"I'm thinking fine." She met his eyes squarely. "I just didn't choose a good time. I'm sorry for that...but I don't regret for what I feel for you, or what we shared together."

"Yeah, well, when you get home, you'll be back to wanting a house in the country and a swing set in the backyard. Babies. And a man who'll give 'em to you."

She opened her mouth to say something else, then closed it. Gabe saw the fragile vulnerability in her face, the hurt in her soft green eyes. Hurt he'd caused, hope he'd smashed. He took a last look at her face, then let himself out.

The hall was deserted and silent. So silent he could have sworn he heard his heart, beating, beating.

He'd been honest with her. Not intentionally unkind. She was prone to believing in illusions and white knights. She'd only get hurt worse if she believed those things with him. Nothing but blunt honesty had a prayer of getting through to Rebecca, yet he still felt a thick, ugly lump clog his throat.

She was the moonbeams and sunshine he'd wanted to believe in—once upon a time. Gabe was uneasy with any fairy-tale words like *love,* but he didn't try to deny there were things he loved about her. He wanted her to have the right to be exactly what she was—a damn fool, an altruistic idealist, a believer in dreams.

The only way that could happen was if he protected her. Not from outside danger. From him.

There was no chance he could be the man she needed. The man she wanted in her life. And Gabe knew it.

Stabbing had always been Rebecca's favorite murder method. She'd killed a few people with poison, used an old British Sten gun another time, ruthlessly drowned a couple, thrown a few more off cliffs. On her computer at home, though, was a suspense book, almost finished, in which the villain favored a silver dagger. Stabbing took a much more gruesome, vicious, face-to-face evil. Stabbing was so much more *personal.* Stabbing was so much more fun.

One book reviewer, Rebecca recalled, had given her kudos for having a deliciously wicked mind. Sheesh, she hoped she did. But that was fiction. In real life, she suffered guilt when she killed a mosquito, and had positively never aspired to meet anyone who could be a murderer—or murderess.

She buttoned her Dobby-weave cream shirt, tucked it into khaki slacks, then pushed her feet into hiking tennies. Her head was pounding and her stomach was queasy. This was the third outfit she'd tried on—which stressed the limit of choices available in her suitcase. Considering how many hours she spent creating greedy, violent killers, she had no idea what the proper dress attire was to meet a potential real one.

Shamelessly cheerful morning sun splashed through the window as she grabbed a hairbrush. Her hair wanted to curl every which way, which was hardly a shock. She'd never had a bad hair day, more like a bad hair life, but debating whether to pull the mop back with barrettes struck her as certifiable. She let it hang.

She reminded herself—again—that because Monica Malone had been stabbed with a letter knife was no reason to assume that Tammy had done the murderous deed. There was no proof Tammy had been in the house at the time of Monica's murder. No evidence that she'd ever touched that letter opener.

And all along, Rebecca had had the niggling intuition that there was some connection between this Tammy and her family, but as Gabe incessantly reminded her, she did have an active imagination. That hunch had never been born out with a single fact.

For that matter, if Gabe really believed Ms. Diller was guilty, Rebecca strongly suspected he'd have found some nasty, nefarious way to kibosh this meeting. Gabe just thought this Diller babe was your average untrustworthy criminal—pond scum, not safe company—but with a potentially valid link to Monica that could save Jake's behind. Rebecca knew Gabe didn't really believe in her brother's innocence, any more than anyone else. And though the rest of the family thought Jake was innocent, they were willing to let Jake's lawyers get him off. Rebecca, however, wasn't about to take any chances with Jake's freedom.

Her brother was emotionally, mentally, ethically and in every other way incapable of stabbing that woman. Rebecca knew that positively. But if Jake hadn't done the slaying, someone else had. And right now the only alternative suspect who'd surfaced anywhere on the planet was Tammy.

The lady who—Rebecca glanced at her watch—she was supposed to meet precisely three hours from now.

She tossed down the hairbrush, applied lipstick, blush, started hooking her mother's charm bracelet on her wrist—no way she was leaving without that good-luck talisman today—and considered whether she had time to throw up. A legion of kamikaze butterflies were diving in her stomach, and every single one of them was nauseous. Their vote was unanimous...but Gabe was due. Overdue by two minutes, in fact.

Gabe rapped on the door before she had conquered the bracelet's clasp. The instant she let him in, his gaze scored the length of her as if he were a daddy dog examining his wayward baby for fleas. "You feel okay? You sleep all right? You ready for this?"

"I couldn't be feeling better, and I'm raring to go." She meant to sound reassuring, but abruptly discovered that she didn't have to sell him any fibs. Her stomach immediately settled down at the look of him—even if her pulse was suddenly racing like a manic battery.

Gabe's attire was casual—camp shirt, jeans, a lightweight aviator jacket. Whether dressed casually or formally, he always managed to look a ton more put-together than she did. His shirts stayed tucked; his hair stayed brushed. His cheeks were fresh-shaven, she noticed, but her heart flip-flopped at the velvet shadows under his eyes. He hadn't forgotten the night before.

Neither had she.

Maybe she'd worriedly suspected before last night that she was falling in love with him. But now she knew. Forget all that confounded clawing desire; she was embarrassed at how abandonedly she'd thrown herself at him the night before. The chemistry was compelling and powerful, but it was only one symptom of this particular disease. Her mind turned to butter just from being near him, and her knees turned to noodles. The damn man had captured a corner of her heart and clenched it in a big, soft fist.

"I'm still not easy about letting you do this," he said darkly.

"Let me give you a tip, love bug. Don't use the words *let* or *allow* around a woman today, and you'll save yourself a shiner."

He leaned one shoulder against the door jamb. "I wouldn't be talking to other women the way I talk to you. This isn't about gender. Some people are gorillas, some lambs. You're gonna be a lamb till the day you die."

"Well, that's possibly the truth, but if you think for a minute, you'll realize that my being a lamb is a mighty advantage." She grabbed her purse, and the scrap of paper holding directions that Tammy had given her the night before, and then zoomed past him down the hall, toward the elevator. "There's nothing to worry about. Trust me—I'm the worst coward you'll ever know. If you think I'd do anything to provoke our dear Ms. Diller, you're out of your mind."

Gabe closed the door and chased after her. Both of them reached to punch the elevator button at the same time. "I believe that the same way I swallow politicians' promises. You're not only no coward, you've taken one reckless risk after another from the day I met you. And this is one afternoon I don't want you to take *any* risks. You remember everything we talked about last night? You cut out of there if you even sense a problem. If you even smell it. If you even feel uneasy."

The elevator doors whooshed open. By the time she stepped in, her eyes sparkled with devilment. "Gabe, Gabe, Gabe...don't tell me you're starting to believe in instincts and intuition? You're not advising me to follow my gut *feelings,* are you?"

Gabe sighed, heavily and loudly. "When you start out this sassy, God knows how I'm gonna be able to deal with you by the end of the day."

Efficient as a marine sergeant, he drilled her on the plans they'd discussed yesterday, where he'd be, where and when they'd meet up, the whole kaboodle. He had a map for her, marked up with yellow marker, too. Instead of sleeping the night before, he'd apparently driven out to the location set up by Tammy and checked out the whole lay of the land.

By the time he finished his whole lethal list of orders, they'd exited the elevator and passed through the lobby, and were nearing a restaurant. Before pushing through those doors, though, he slapped a key in her hand.

"What's this?"

"I rented you a car. A black Mazda RX-7."

She blinked. "A plain old cute little Chevy would have done me."

"Maybe. But if you decide you want to cut out, you put your foot on *that* accelerator, it'll move."

Rebecca hadn't even tried to get a word in before then. It'd have been like interrupting a surgeon with a scalpel in his hands. Gabe was in his element organizing and planning, and, truth to tell, he was wonderful at it. His last comment, though, she simply couldn't let pass.

She put her hand on his elbow to catch his attention, and then said softly, quietly, "I don't cut out on trouble, Gabe. I may be scared, I may throw up, I may bungle things and handle them badly. But I don't cut out when there's a problem. You can take that to the bank."

Nine

Although the drive from Las Vegas to the Red Rock Canyon lands was only fifteen miles, it might as well have been the distance to another planet. Civilized glitter and glitz first turned into desert, then into wild, raw, mountainous rock country.

For a tourist tired of losing money at blackjack, Gabe could easily see how a nature trek to the canyons would be a refreshing change. Somehow, though, he suspected Tammy Diller had chosen the location for entirely different reasons.

He scratched his chin...very, very quietly. Tammy had already arrived—in a pale yellow Cadillac with rental plates. He'd already taken a long, slow drink of her, and he didn't like the taste.

Although Ms. Diller didn't know it, Gabe was twenty-five feet above her, lying flat on an itchy, dusty rock slab. It was an unbeatable vantage point, close enough for him to even hear the conversation directly, if he was lucky. But that was assuming he didn't fry first.

Tammy had suggested Rebecca meet her at the picnic site inside the recreation park area. Technically, it was a logical, innocuous, peaceful spot for a private chat—and apparently safe, because it was public. Only on a midweek afternoon, with a relentless sun reflecting off the striated, naked rocks, it was bone-baking hot. There wasn't a body anywhere around—no birds, no critters, and for sure no other humans.

Gabe had brought a canteen, but he didn't dare risk a drink for fear of making noise. And he was pretty sure a geologist would find the countryside a paradise—a few gnarled cottonwood trees cast some blessed shade on the picnic site, but beyond that, salmon-and-apricot rock formations rose in eerie spires and shapes, backdropped by multicolored sandstone bluffs. A lot of schist in the canyon walls, Gabe guessed, because they were striated with garnet and minerals and iron and all kinds of striking color.

He didn't give a damn about the geology or the beauty. When he left his car miles back and hiked to the site, it had kept ragging on his nerves, how isolated the location was. No population. No buildings in sight. A fine spot to do anything and not risk getting caught.

And the lady below kept pushing his personal alarm buttons. Tammy had arrived twenty minutes ahead of the scheduled meeting, so he'd had ample time to study her. Big hair. Brown, shoulder-length; he supposed another woman would call the style artful. He called it cheap.

Her makeup was cheap, too, and she seemed to favor applying it by the pound on her eyes. Long legs—not bad. A fussy-gussy blouse dripped lace over a significantly stacked upper deck. Gabe thought she was probably trying to look innocent and trustworthy with that lace getup, and the clothes cost enough; it was the way she wore them, the way she walked. She was trash. Gabe suspected Rebecca'd yank his chain with a long feminist harangue if he used that sexist term around her.

But she was. Trash to the bone. Ten miles of rough road in those cold eyes. Nothing wrong with the face—the woman was essentially pretty—but the expression was harder than shoe leather. She was edgy enough to keep jumping at sounds that weren't there—and he wasn't making any.

They both heard the purr of a car engine—it had to be Rebecca coming. Gabe's muscles clenched, but he never cut his eyes from Tammy. Faster than bad news, she crushed a cigarette, tossed out the gum, wrapped a scarf around her hair, put on a big pair of sunglasses and rearranged her face into a calm, cool model of serenity.

Rebecca braked the black Mazda right next to Tammy's car and climbed out. *Okay, Red,* Gabe thought. *Just be good for me this one time. Do what we said. Chitchat, but no more. Don't bring up Monica, don't bring up your brother, and for God's sake, don't bring up murder. You can risk your neck tomorrow, shorty, I promise, but just be careful this one time, okay? Just this once...*

"Ms. Diller?" Rebecca obviously spotted the

other woman immediately, because she strode straight toward her. God, she was like a ray of clean, natural sunshine compared to that road-hard piece of work.

Only something was wrong. Gabe didn't know what, couldn't guess what. But he knew Rebecca's body—intimately. It might not have been apparent to anyone else, but her shoulders suddenly tensed up— even the muscles in her minuscule fanny tightened— and her smile suddenly looked like an artificial "company" smile.

Alarm buttons clanged all through Gabe's nervous system. He'd plugged into his computer system in the wee small hours, hoping that more background on Tammy would finally surface—or that another suspect might pan out. Monica had no shortage of enemies. He'd had his staff checking every name Kate and Jake Fortune had come up with. Reams of information were still emerging from that investigation—some easier to dig up than others. But no pay dirt. Nothing sure that Gabe could have used to justify calling off this whole crazy meeting.

Now, though, he wished he'd said to hell with logic and facts and just done it. Called it off. If Rebecca was shook up at the look of the woman, there was obviously something he didn't know. Gabe liked surprises. But not concerning Rebecca, and, dammit, not concerning her safety.

Still, she seemed to recover quickly from that first startled stiffness. Her hand extended to Tammy and, as was typical of Ms. Pollyanna, her voice held warmth and the natural bubble of enthusiasm. "Hi there! What an incredibly beautiful place. And I really appreciate your taking the time to meet me."

Tammy clasped her hand with a smile brighter than fool's gold. Her southern accent sounded authentic, but her voice dripped more sugar than Gabe had ever heard in New Orleans. "I just always loved this area, and it seemed like such an ideal place to relax. It's awfully hard to find a quiet spot in Vegas."

"You're not kidding."

Gabe missed some of the start-up chitchat. Tammy's back was to him, making it easy enough to spy, which had originally been all he thought he'd ever be able to do—get close enough to watch her, close enough to move fast if there seemed any threat to Rebecca. It was an unexpected gift that sound carried so well in that total quiet, crystal-sharp air, but the women's voices blurred if they moved at all. Women being women, they couldn't stand still. Gabe was trying not to breathe, trying to ignore the buzzing itch at his nape, trying to forget the heat and the gritty pointed rock stabbing his chest.

They seemed to be just companionably chatting, nothing tense, nothing worrisome, judging from the glimpses he could catch of Rebecca's face. She was chattering like a gregarious, friendly magpie, and Gabe thought *Attagirl, you're doing this just right, shorty.*

Then they ambled a little closer to him, and out of nowhere Tammy cocked her innocent little head and got down to business. "Everywhere I went yesterday, someone seemed to say you were looking for me. With us not knowing each other from Adam, I couldn't imagine why."

"Well, if I can be frank with you..."

A sudden scissor of alarm sheared up Gabe's spine. It was that guileless tone of Rebecca's. The last time he heard it, she'd been blithely, gently informing him that she never cut and ran on a problem. And, dammit, he *knew* that. She'd more than proved that there was no harebrained thing she wouldn't do to help her brother. She never backed down from a problem because of risk. And she'd intimately taught him that lesson the night before—with the risks she'd taken with him.

Every moment, every touch and wild, sweeping caress from last night echoed in his mind. And that scissor of alarm clipping up his spine suddenly started slashing at him at warp speed.

"Of course you can be frank with me, honey," Tammy reassured her.

"Well...I don't know if you read about Monica Malone's murder in the newspapers, but my brother Jake was charged with the crime. I found a copy of a letter that Monica wrote to you around the time of her death. I don't have any idea what connection you had with her, but I was just hoping you could help me. I'm looking for something, anything, that might help me clear my brother.''

Gabe's heart stopped. His throat went drier than the Sahara at high noon. Not only had he lectured her a dozen times, she'd agreed, she'd understood that the one subject she mustn't bring up with Tammy was Monica's murder. It was the same as inviting the woman to see Rebecca as a serious threat. He thought, *Damn you, Red, don't you dare say one more word.*

For that instant, he couldn't see Tammy's face, but she raised her hands in an innocent gesture. ''I knew, of course, about Monica's death, because she was such a public Hollywood figure, and it was everywhere in the media. But, gosh, I sure never knew her personally—''

''But there was a letter to you,'' Rebecca persisted firmly.

Gabe's heart started beating again—in fast, sick, worried thuds. Enough adrenaline pumped through his veins to threaten an OD rush. He mentally debated whether, when he caught up with shorty again, he'd boil her in oil, tie her to a post on an anthill, or drown her. All those options were so tempting, it was tough to pin down a favorite. But that was for later, and as of that moment, his gaze narrowed on Tammy. He didn't plan to let the lady out of his sight, even to blink.

''Well, you're so right about my getting that letter from Monica,'' Tammy smoothly admitted. ''Really took me by surprise. As you can probably guess, with my looks and all, I've done some modeling. I thought Monica must have been contacting me because of that. I read somewhere that she had an affiliation with your family's cosmetic company, and for just a real short spurt here, I was in between jobs. Truthfully, though, I don't know. I was working after that, so I just never had a chance to follow up with that letter.''

''Well, shoot,'' Rebecca said. ''I'd really hoped you might have some concrete ideas I could follow up, some connection with someone to Monica besides my brother.''

''Afraid not, sugar. I never met the woman. Not that I didn't feel sympathy... I mean, how terrible, that an old Hollywood star would get murdered like that, stabbed with a jeweled letter opener, just like in some movie. Shocking to believe anyone could do such a thing, isn't it? Just gives me the willies even to think about it.''

Hell. Something new was wrong. Rebecca came up with a response, but the color washed out of her face and she suddenly clenched her hands. The tense movement made the bracelet on her wrist jangle.

Tammy said something about the charm bracelet, and the conversation got sidetracked to jewelry, an obvious effort by Ms. Diller to switch the subject from Monica. Both women made itchy movements. Both plucked car keys from their purses and dangled them, still chatting. Neither wanted to pursue this "meeting" any longer, but neither seemed to know how to cut it off quickly, either.

Gabe told himself it was okay to breathe. Nothing more was going to happen at this instant. Tammy would have, could have, made some move on Rebecca if she was going to. It was also possible that, on her terms, the meeting had gone well. She'd had the chance to find out what Rebecca wanted, and with any luck even believed that she'd sold Rebecca her whole fine, forthright, honest act.

Regretfully, though, Gabe had never believed the easy, happy endings in fairy tales.

Lying there still was driving him nuts. He wanted to climb off that rock, hike back to his car and *get* there before Tammy took off. Unfortunately, he couldn't budge without making noises that would reveal his presence. Patience was required until Tammy left, but his mind was spinning ahead, planning. Even if he ended up long minutes behind Ms. Diller, following her wouldn't be that hard. He could catch up. A limited number of roads led out of this canyon area, and that pretty yellow Cadillac would be easy to spot on the highway.

He didn't know where Tammy was going from here, but every gut instinct warned him to find out. Following her, seeing what she did next, was the best way to find out if she was upset or intended to act on the information she'd learned from Rebecca.

Later, he'd deal with shorty.

* * *

Rebecca's hands were slippery on the steering wheel, damp from both nerves and excitement. The black Mazda zoomed along the highway back to Vegas, galloping past ninety before she realized how hard her foot was smashed on the accelerator. It was like trying to hold a Thoroughbred back at the Derby. The baby wanted to run like the wind.

So did Rebecca.

She'd almost had a heart attack when she first saw Tammy. Though the woman had tried to make herself look different, she had an incredible likeness to Rebecca's older sister, Lindsay. The instant she realized that, a dozen puzzle pieces had suddenly clicked together.

Tammy Diller was just a fake name for Tracey Ducet. She'd *known* there was something about the name that rang a memory bell for her. She'd known the whole story of the woman who tried to pass herself off as Lindsay's missing twin more than a year before—the whole family had been up in arms. She just hadn't made the connection until she laid eyes on the woman.

Tracey/Tammy had five tons of gall to risk meeting with her. No disguise was that good. But arrogance—and gambling for big stakes—was clearly part of the woman's makeup.

As if recognizing her weren't heart attack enough, Rebecca almost had a second one when Tracey/Tammy mentioned Monica's being stabbed. The murder weapon had never been mentioned in any of the papers or tabloids. The police had guarded that information tighter than gold. They'd had ample up-front evidence to charge her brother with the crime, but there had still been some unanswered questions—notably how many fingerprints had been on the antique jeweled letter opener, and who else those smudged prints might belong to. Because of the Fortune name, it was going to be a big trial, and they were scared of screwing it up. Information that could directly affect the trial had been ruthlessly kept out of the press.

But Tracey had known. She'd *said*. She'd commented on both the stabbing and the jeweled letter opener.

That was all Rebecca had needed to hear to be sure Ms. Ducet was the actual murderess. She couldn't wait to get away from the woman. Couldn't wait to get back to the hotel, to tell Gabe—and the police—that they had some real information they could use to nail the woman. And, please God, to free her brother from that horrible jail cell.

The highway had been relatively empty, but heavier traffic clustered near town, and Rebecca was so distracted she took several wrong turns. It was pretty hard to get lost in Vegas—the major hotels shot up to cloud height, with their names in clear lights—but she simply wasn't concentrating on directions.

Eventually she located Circus Circus, mentally kicking herself for wasting time, when all she wanted was to hurry. She aimed up the multi-level parking facility, yanked a slip of paper from the machine and blinked in the sudden cool shade after all that blinding sun. She was supposed to meet Gabe in her room. With her lollygagging around and getting lost, it was hard to guess if he could have arrived before she did.

She couldn't wait to filch a pop—her dry throat was begging for one—and to see his face when she spilled her news about Tracey. She knew he'd listen seriously, because Gabe never failed to be objective about his work. And there'd be an eensy glint of miffed male pride in his eyes, because, poor baby, his ego really hated it when she discovered something that he hadn't. But Rebecca knew he'd be pleased, for her, with her. Maybe pleased enough to forget that she'd ignored all his orders regarding how that meeting with Tracey was supposed to go.

Gabe should know by now—especially after last night—that she really didn't take orders or warnings well. Her heart suddenly clenched. When someone she cared about was involved, she had a disgracefully long history of ignoring the rules—but never as many rules as she'd broken with Gabe, and never at such risk to her heart.

Now, though, was no time to dwell on that. Because the parking garage on the first level was packed, she had to circle up to the next floor. Finally she found a spot for the Mazda to squeeze into. She cut the engine, and grabbed the key and her purse. Her pulse was racing like a runaway freight train, and her nerves were a frantic jumble of anticipation at the thought of seeing Gabe and the edgy rush and excitement left over from the meeting with Tracey.

She stepped out of the car and locked it, then turned around. There was nothing but silent, oppressive concrete in every direction, the parking ramp gloomy and dim. Momentarily she was disoriented, unsure where the exit was or how to get back into the hotel.

"Hey!"

She turned her head at the sound of the man's voice. In that first instant, it didn't seem that odd that a stranger would be calling her—Vegas was a tourist place, so strangers naturally picked up conversations with fellow strangers almost everywhere. And the first thing she saw was the man's smile. Her mind registered other details, like that he was tall and blond and wearing innocuously nice tourist clothes, a nice-looking youngish man in his mid-thirties...and suddenly her memory spun.

Tammy had a sidekick-man friend. It was one of the reasons she should have connected Tammy to Tracey before, because a boyfriend had been part of the scam Tracey'd tried to pull on the Fortune family the first time. Dwayne, Wayne, something like that... But even as fast as her pulse recognized danger, it was too late. In those few seconds, he'd already jogged up to her. Even in the murky light, his boyish smile and polite, cordial expression were very clear. And then she caught the bright, pretty glint of silver in his right hand. He was still smiling when he raised the blade.

There was no one in sight, no sound or movement indicating that anyone else was remotely nearby. That didn't stop Rebecca. She sucked in a lungful of air, with every intention of screaming loud enough to wake the dead.

The scream never made it. She barely yelped out a squeak before he was on her, whipping her around, yanking her arm painfully tight behind her back. The smell of a thick, cloying men's cologne assaulted her nostrils. She suddenly couldn't breathe. The silver blade shot gorgeous, shiny reflections of light on the far concrete wall, but the knife was pressed right at her throat. She could feel the point. She could feel panic, bubbling up like a sudden, inescapable tidal wave.

The name Wayne Potts shot into her head like a bullet. A totally useless bullet, because putting together all the details was no weapon that could protect her now. She should have been more careful. She should have trusted her intuition, and tried harder to remember why the whole Tammy Diller/boyfriend story bothered her long before this. But all those should-have-beens were nothing compared to the feel of that cool, smooth blade against her throat.

"You're late, Ms. Fortune. I expected you a good twenty minutes ago, and was starting to wonder what the hell could have happened to you. Did you get lost? It should only have taken you so much time to drive a short fifteen miles.''

He wanted to talk? She was more in the mood to wet her pants, vent a solid case of hysteria, dissolve in a puddle of terror...maybe all three at the same time. There was no chance she could concentrate on anything but that knife, so close, so close, already pricking the skin of her throat. On the other hand, as long as he was talking, she wasn't dying. "How did you know my name?"

"Hardly a challenge. Car phones are a wonderful technological boon, don't you think? I heard all about you. Tracey couldn't wait to tell me all about you. And you talked a good game, honey. You had Tracey convinced you were as naive as a newborn kitten...and there was no doubt in her mind that you believed every word she said. I learned real young to recognize a counterfeit dollar.''

He yanked her arm again, making her eyes burn with hot tears. Beneath the thick smell of men's cologne was the stench of his sweat. Excitement sweat. He liked this, she understood with a primal instinct. She couldn't make her voice sound real, even to save her life. "I don't understand. I don't have any idea what you're talking about. I never heard of any Tracey—''

His chuckle was without humor, right next to her ear. "Good try, babe. But I wouldn't try lying to a pro. You recognized Tracey right off the bat, didn't you? Of course you did. She looks just like your older sister. I told Tracey that meeting idea was stupid, but she just wouldn't listen, said it was too important for us to find out what you knew. And we found out that answer, didn't we? You know too damn much—''

From nowhere came the sudden sound of tires screeching and squealing. The interruption was enough to distract him into looking up. Not Rebecca. When he jerked up his head, the knife at her throat tightened, stung, the blade drawing blood she could feel. There was no way she could risk moving her head even a fraction. But the corner of her eyes caught the shiny white top of Gabe's rental car, racing hell-bent for leather around the curve of the parking ramp.

The engine zoomed, accelerating like a jet preparing for takeoff, coming, coming, as if the car impossibly intended to mow down them both. Instead, just out of her vision, she heard an ear-shattering, metal-screaming crunch as Gabe crashed straight into the car parked next to hers. His wheels were still spinning, his engine still running, when the driver's door shot open.

The whole thing didn't take seconds. If Wayne had had a brain, he'd undoubtedly have realized that he was holding the highest card, and his best move was to hold on even tighter to her. But there was no time for anything but an instinctive response, and Wayne's instinctive response to a problem was to run.

The blade skimmed her throat, biting and stinging like holy blazes, but then he pushed her, roughly, and she was suddenly free. Her abdomen slammed into the hood of a car, bruising hard. For a second, she couldn't catch her balance, couldn't catch her breath, and all she really wanted to do was let her knees buckle and have a nice, noisy case of hysterics—but then she saw Gabe. He was moving like a blue streak, something terrifying in his black eyes.

"Gabe, he has a knife!" she yelled, but it was like talking to a jet. A deaf jet. He seemed to fly on top of Wayne in a tackle that left them both scrambling on the cement. The silver knife arced in the air, fell and skittered under some stranger's car, out of sight.

Gabe was already twisting Wayne around, yanking him up, pulling back one arm. He buried a fist in his diaphragm, making Wayne double over with a loud *whoomph*. Gabe grabbed him again, as if the man didn't weigh any more than a dog, clapped both hands hard over his ears and then slammed him, hard, against the cement wall. Wayne started screaming and crying, trying to scramble away, trying to protect himself.

Rebecca froze, her hand on her stomach, too shook up to have a clue what to do for an instant—help Gabe, obviously, but *how?* Get the knife? Call the police, but how could she leave him?

And then the sound of a car engine added to the confusion of noise—it was just some tourists, an older couple who'd unwittingly chosen that moment to need a parking place. Rebecca stumbled into the middle of the lane to block their path, waving wildly at the driver to make him stop. Two sets of eyes stared at her through the windshield, looking both bewildered and startled.

"Just leave the car here and call the police—please!" she yelled at them. When they still sat there, looking shell-shocked, she yelped again, "*Go!* Go into the hotel and call the police! Please!"

Both the man and his wife hustled out of their doors then. The white-haired gentleman had the presence of mind to ask her, "Are you all right?"

"I'm fine, I'm fine," she assured them, but once they quickly ducked out of sight, she thought she'd never been less "fine" in her entire life. As she whirled around to see Gabe's fist slam into Wayne's stomach again, she thought Gabe was hardly fine, either.

He was scaring her. Maybe it was the other man who was taking the battering, but some nameless feminine instinct sensed that Gabe was taking a different kind of beating. She'd never seen him so dead cold before. She'd never seen a hint of violence, in his eyes, in his actions. Some instinct made her call out, "Gabe, he didn't hurt me! I'm all right."

There was no immediate response. She wasn't sure if he heard her, if he saw her, if he even knew she was there. She jogged toward the men, still unsure what to do, what she could do, what needed doing. The closer she came, the clearer she could see the dark rage in Gabe's expression. God, that look was imprinted on her mind like a haunting nightmare.

"I'm okay. He didn't hurt me," she repeated, and then repeated it again.

Maybe he finally heard her. Maybe he finally just stopped. Wayne slumped against the concrete wall, then sank to his knees on the ground, gasping and crying. For an instant, he didn't seem to believe that Gabe had quit hitting him and was letting him be, but Wayne wasn't going anywhere, anyway.

Metal doors slapped open. People started running. Rebecca saw uniformed security people racing toward them, heard the wail of a siren, and closed her eyes for a second to try, just try, to catch her breath.

When she opened them, in spite of all the noise and shouts and milling bodies, all she really saw were Gabe's eyes from a half-dozen feet away, meeting hers as if there weren't a soul in the entire universe but the two of them.

Ten

Gabe rapped his knuckles on the bathroom door. "Room service."

He heard a muffled chuckle. "At the moment, room service would be stuck with more than an eyeful. I'm still in the bathtub, Gabe. Be out in two shakes."

"No reason to come out. The longer you soak, the better. But this chicken soup's gonna get cold. Why don't you just grab one of those extra towels and wrap it around you for a cover-up, so I can bring the food in?"

"You mean eat dinner in the bathtub?" He heard her sigh. "What a decadent, disgraceful, shamelessly lazy idea."

"Does that mean no, or does that mean that you've got the towel on?"

"It means I've got the towel on and I can't believe you managed to worm chicken soup out of room service."

He had to balance the tray on one arm to open the door. Fragrant, warm steam billowed out, carrying some exotic, sensual, pure-female scent like jasmine. The scent awakened every masculine hormone, but, being as good as a monk, Gabe kept his eyes averted from Rebecca's body. There was no point in telling shorty that he'd have found some way to bribe his way in there if the chicken soup hadn't worked. Even less point in telling her that he was damned determined to see her naked.

Rebecca had told him—a dozen times now—that she was "fine." He'd seen the long, skinny cut that son of a bitch had put on her neck. Before, though, she'd been clothed from long sleeves to ankles, and there'd been no way to know if the bastard had injured her anywhere else. Trusting Rebecca to admit to being hurt was like waiting for cows to waltz.

"Just so you know I haven't got these waiter skills down pat yet. If I end up spilling chicken soup in the bathtub, you can forgo the tip." With his gaze still averted, he set up the tray on the sink, then booted the door closed so that she wouldn't lose any more of that hotter-than-sex steamy heat.

"Spoon first, ma'am. Then the bowl. They gave you a linen napkin for this elegant meal, but personally I think it'd look pretty silly tied under your chin. We'll just put it within reach. And seeing as it's only me, I'm making the announcement right now that it's okay if you slurp."

He earned a couple of chuckles from her, but they didn't sound like Rebecca's laugh and they didn't last long. Still playing the virtuous gentleman, he managed to hunker over the tub and serve the food without once peeking a glance below her neck.

Once she dived into that bowl of soup, though, he used the toilet seat for a chair and parked there. The heat gave him an excuse to yank off his shoes and socks, but that was only to look busy. The corners of both his eyes were on her tighter than the skin on a peach.

Her curly hair had turned into a wild garnet-and-cinnamon halo in the humidity. Damp strands clung to her brow and nape. She'd modestly knotted the wet towel, concealing even the swell of her breasts, but those hotel towels were thankfully skimpy by nature.

Her skin was whiter than virgin snow, and he could see plenty of it. The red pinprick knife slice on her throat made his gut clench and twist. So did the ink-blot bruise on her thigh, and there were two more on her forearms—blotches of bruises like hand-prints. That creep had mauled her around really hard. It could have been worse, Gabe kept telling himself. But it *was* worse.

Where Rebecca was hurt the most didn't show up in physical scrapes and bruises. It was in her eyes. There was no sass in those forest green eyes tonight, no sparkle; she dived into the soup with a decent appetite, but her gaze skittered around like a cornered rabbit's, landing on nothing, settling on nothing. She was still seeing fear. She was still *feeling* fear.

It'd been three hours since the cops cuffed Wayne and taken him away. All the cops' questions had been answered, all the commotion and hoopla had long ago died down. Shorty'd stayed real cool, real calm. She didn't seem to know that when you went through something traumatic and terrifying, sooner or later there was always some reaction.

"How'd you even *think* of chicken soup? Have you been secretly hiding a maternal caretaking streak all this time?" she teased him.

"Now don't go leaping to any rash, insulting conclusions. I just couldn't think of anything else but soup. I didn't figure you'd be in any mood to eat anything heavy."

"Well, you did good. No way I could have handled a steak, not tonight.... Do you think the police have caught Tracey by now?"

Back to that. They'd already covered that ground, but Gabe wasn't surprised she couldn't let it go. "I think the chances are excellent. Tracey had no way to know what happened to her sidekick, no reason to hide or guess anything had gone wrong. She was likely headed straight home to connect fast with Wayne. I'd think the cops would have had a really easy job tracking her down."

"You think I should call my mom again?"

More old ground. "I'd guess that Kate hasn't been off Ma Bell since you called her the first time. Like I told you, she had an intuition about the Tammy Diller/Tracey Ducet connection—enough to make me plug the Ducet name into the computer banks. The woman was just so skilled with changing names and identities that tracking her background took time.

We'd have gotten it. But not half as fast as the way this played out. And the point is that knowing your mother, she'll be on this like a bear stirring a hornet's nest. I'd bet the bank that Kate has already—long and loudly—yanked the tie on every lawyer involved in your brother's case."

"It's going to make a difference, isn't it, Gabe?"

"You bet it is."

"I can't say I ever want to meet up with Wayne-boy and a knife again. Or that awful woman. But it was worth it. If something like this hadn't happened—something real, something concrete—we'd never have been able to force Tracey's hand. Whatever illegal stuff she was involved in, there just wasn't a connection to Monica's murder. Not a provable connection, before this."

"Yeah." Gabe had to bite out the single syllable. What he wanted to do was lecture her for ignoring him and taking such damn fool insane risks. It would wait. He'd get around to yelling at her, because she sure as spit deserved it. But not tonight; definitely, definitely, not tonight.

Doe-soft eyes lanced on his face. The damn woman didn't even know how haunted they were. "I still don't understand how you found me so fast."

They'd trekked down that conversational road before, too, but Gabe patiently covered it again. "My intention was to follow Tammy/Tracey, like I told you, because I could see right away in that meeting that something scared you about her. My first thought was to track her, find out exactly where she was going and what she planned to do next. And that's what I was doing, until I saw her reach down, while she was driving, and put a cellular phone to her ear. The only person she would likely be calling was her sidekick. And if she was reporting in to her boyfriend, that meant—as far as I was concerned—that whatever she was doing dropped on the priority scale. He was the immediate and potential threat to you."

She finished eating, falling silent. When the bowl was empty, he scooped up the dish and spoon and plopped them on the tray. He could feel her eyes following him, though. For several minutes her gaze had been mapping his face, every line, every boned ridge and hollow.

"You want to get it off your chest or not?" he asked bluntly.

"Get what off my chest?"

"Damned if I know. We've rehashed what happened...or most of what happened...a half-dozen times now. But you seem to be avoiding talking about something on your mind, like it'd bite you."

She met his eyes again, swallowed, and then slowly nodded. "I was frightened when you were hitting Wayne. I was frightened you wouldn't stop."

"He tried to kill you."

"He was a pipsqueak. A weakling. No match for you."

"He tried to kill you," Gabe repeated, and then sighed. To him, that was the period at the end of the sentence. Any man would understand that, but Rebecca just wasn't going to think like a man in this lifetime. "If you think I get a thrill out of violence, you can rest your mind, Red. I hate it. And investigating work is nothing like you see on TV, nothing like the work I did in the military, either. It's damn rare I can't find a better way to solve a problem than raising my fists. But I know how. And there's a time and place when that's the only choice."

"But you wanted to hurt him," she said uneasily.

"You bet I did. And I know how to hurt a man. But contrary to what you seem to be scared of, I was in control, would never have allowed myself to lose that control. We want both those characters alive and well—both so the cops can grill them and so they can testify in court. I was never going to hurt him in any way that would have jeopardized your brother's situation."

"And what if my brother's legal problems weren't involved?"

Gabe sighed. Again. "Shorty, I can't give you an answer that you're gonna like. That jerk wasn't playing pattycake. He was threatening your life. If you wanted me to slap his hands and say no, no, that was never going to happen. There is no guarantee what the law will do with Wayne, so I wanted to make sure he clearly understood that he really, really didn't want to go near you again. Wayne is no nice-boy accountant. He's one of those animals that never evolved. And when you're trying to communicate to an animal, sometimes being polite just doesn't get the job done."

"All right. I get you. I understand. But it still made me sick that you had to hit someone because of me."

Gabe didn't know what to say to that. Something was going screwy in this whole discussion. She was listening, meeting his eyes straight and true, but something about the way she looked at him was stirring his hormones into a sizzling stew.

His conscience needed to give him a whomp upside the head. The last thing on earth that should have been on his mind was sex. She was bruised and shook up, her skin still looking paler than fragile china, those eyes still anxious and way too vulnerable. It was an utterly illogical time to discover that she was incomparably beautiful. An even more illogical and irrational time to feel desire…much less desire so strong it lashed around his nerves like a hot whip.

"Gabe?"

"What?" He scrubbed a hand over his face, willing his wayward thoughts to disappear. The source of all these stupid, tumultuous emotions was obvious. He'd been scared out of his mind when he saw that bastard with a knife at her throat. He'd come damn close to losing her. Too close. But he hadn't. She was safe; she was okay; she was with him. And if he could just get that obvious truth to his head, maybe he could make his heart stop pounding and settle down.

"It took you a long time," Rebecca said, "but you finally believe in my brother's innocence, don't you?"

That whole subject was safer ground. "Yeah, I do. Not that it ever mattered what I believed. What mattered was that we were able to scare up evidence that pointed to another viable suspect. It's impossible to know if Tracey'll go down for the murder—I'm afraid that's completely dependent on what the cops stir up after questioning her. But a jury'd have to be deaf and dumb not to see the reasonable doubt as far as your brother's concerned."

Rebecca frowned. "What you believe does matter. To me. No one believed me about Jake's innocence before."

"Yeah, well, you run pretty heavy in the intuition department, shorty. Some people are a little more comfortable trusting facts." He stood up, suddenly feeling as rattled as a caged cougar. This was just no good. The longer he looked at her, the more his mind was stripped bare of common sense. "You're going to turn into a prune if we don't let you out of there. I'll just go in the other room. You got a robe in here?"

Even as he asked, he noticed the white silk kimono thing hanging on the door hook. Picturing her naked body wrapped in that was *not* helping him get his head together.

"Look," he said gruffly. "I'm just going to stick around until I'm sure you're asleep, okay? There's bound to be some brainless sitcom on the tube. And we can order more food if you're still hungry. You can just put your feet up and veg out until you feel like sleeping."

"I'm fine, Gabe."

So she'd said. Several times. But he didn't think so.

Once on the other side of that bathroom door, he got busier than a mother hen. The curtains were open; he reeled them shut. The overhead light was harsh; he flicked it off. He folded down the bedspread, piled some pillows, fiddled with the TV until he found the most innocuous, mindless program on the air, and set the volume on low.

The whole time he was chasing around, his pulse seemed to be beating to incessant low drums. Hitchcock always put drumrolls in a movie, right before some terrifying disaster took place—but this wasn't like that. The disasters had all happened, were all over. He knew Rebecca was upset, that was all. He doubted she'd ever been shaking-hands close to any kind of violence before. He'd be surprised if she didn't have nightmares tonight.

He shoveled a hand through his hair as he glanced around the room. He'd just sit in the far corner, he decided. Physically away from her. There was absolutely no reason to tell shorty he planned to spend the night. She'd just be annoyed. And sooner or later she'd fall asleep, but if and when she had nightmares, then he'd be there.

That drumroll echoed in his pulse again, a dark, slow, insidious pagan rhythm that he couldn't explain. It was...stupid. It wasn't like he'd missed her his whole life. It wasn't like he'd felt a rage beyond sanity when he saw Wayne's hands on her. It wasn't like he couldn't shake the dread-panic feeling that nothing in his life would be right again if he lost her.

He was just having a little trouble settling down tonight. Normally he thrived on stress. Hell's bells, he *loved* stress. It was just knowing that Rebecca was still suffering some upset reactions that had him feeling...edgy. As soon as she was safe and sound and tucked in bed, he'd be fine.

Only when the bathroom door opened and she stepped out in that sin-soft silk kimono, Rebecca didn't even glance at the bed.

She walked straight into his arms.

"I was so scared."

"I know you were."

"I've never been that scared. First with her, Tracey. Those cold eyes—it's like there wasn't a human being with feelings on the other side. I know it doesn't make sense, but I think I was more scared of her than I was of Wayne. And when Wayne grabbed me...Gabe, I just couldn't make my mind believe it. That he really intended to kill me, that any human being could that easily hurt someone else—"

"S'okay. S'okay. You never have to be around

people like that again. No one's gonna hurt you now. It's over."

When she walked out of the bathroom, Rebecca hadn't known it was going to come bubbling, babbling out like this. She hadn't known that she would suddenly feel desperate, for a hug, for physical contact, for the warmth of arms around her. She didn't know those impulses would hit her so fast, so unfightably strong.

Yet needing Gabe—and trusting that he'd be there for her—came as no surprise at all.

His need for her did.

She heard his voice, soothing, quieting, chanting comfort words like a litany...but there was something raw in his voice, raw as a fresh sore. She wondered if Gabe even knew he was hurting. His face was gaunt and silver by the dim light of the flickering television screen, and his eyes were as deep and black as ebony. His arms were wrapped tight around her, his muscles unyieldingly rigid and tense. She thought of wire stretched so tight that it just might break.

His arms suddenly tightened around her in a different way. That long string of comfort words... His voice suddenly trailed off, died into silence. And from nowhere, as if by accident, his mouth was suddenly hovering a breath's distance from hers.

She'd desperately needed a hug. Needed Gabe. But nothing sexual had been on her mind. The stress and fear of the day had simply been explosive. She'd had to let go.

So, it seemed, did he.

His lips whispered down, touched down, then clung. Bald passion had dominated his kisses before. The hint of wild wolf in Gabe had inspired a heady, primitive response in her, but this was more.

His mouth took hers with tenderness, a shattering tenderness that shook her from the inside out. That first kiss was almost desperately soft.

His lips were yielding, warm, clinging the way flames lapped around a fireplace log. No fire could exist without its source of heat. Right then, just then, Rebecca had the vulnerable sensation that she was his only source of heat.

His hands roamed her back, caressing, stroking, as if he were polishing her skin beneath the filmy silk robe, as if he couldn't stop touching her. Canned laughter echoed from the TV, but it was muted, distant. When he suddenly lifted his head, the need she saw in his eyes shocked her.

He hadn't known he was going to kiss her.

She suspected he didn't know yet that they were going to make love.

She did. His head dipped down again. One kiss swirled into another, melted into yet another. Her fingers found his shirt buttons. His hands found their way into her hair, sieving deep, holding her still, holding her, holding her.

Maybe he didn't know he was expressing love, but that was the depth of clear emotion he communicated to her. Not for the first time, Rebecca sensed how much he resembled her brother Jake. He was not a man who could survive being trapped behind bars forever. Sometimes feelings had to be let out. Sometimes, even if you were scared no one else was on the other side of the abyss, you had to take the risk and find out. Denying need never made it go away.

She unlatched his belt, loosened it, flicked open the button at his waist. He was just as busy, slowly sliding the robe off her shoulders, off her arms. The kimono dropped to the floor in a silent *whoosh*.

Fire kindled in his eyes when he saw her bare. His expression turned grave, almost harsh. The silvery light played on his skin as he eased her down on the bed. The mattress was a welcome support for her noodle-knees, for her curling toes, for the shuddering anticipation careening through her veins.

He murmured, "Dammit, Rebecca," but his deep, hoarse voice was like a man's caress.

The man was going to inspire her to wanton savagery, if he wasn't careful. Personally, she was losing all interest in being careful. She thought of the ugliness of the violence he'd grown up with. She thought of how disturbed she'd been when she watched him hit Wayne—not for Wayne, the worm-scum—but for Gabe. She thought of a man who'd kill to protect her, even if it hurt him, even if it echoed everything wrong and painful about his childhood. Gabe was afraid of things, too. Afraid of belonging. Afraid of longing. Afraid of anything soft in his life that he might, damn foolishly, become dependent on.

Well, he was getting soft tonight—whether he was afraid of it or not. He was going to belong to someone.

Her tongue dueled with his in a warm, wet kiss. Fingertips and palms sang down his throat, his shoulders, the thatchy hair on his chest. He touched, too. His hands had a memory of where she was bruised and sore, because he seemed intent on blindly touching those places, erasing where she'd been handled harshly, painting gentleness in those places in his name. And he was gentle. But need was thrumming between them, too, building in rhythm, and his arousal was pulsing hot and heavy against her abdomen.

She pushed at his pants, and earned a rough, low chuckle from him for being so impatient. It was premature, she thought. Gabe hadn't seen yet what a lady could do in a frenzy of impatience—but she did her best to show him. The bedspread crumpled to the carpet. Pillows seemed to fly. Blankets rumpled and rucked. Even rolling with him in every direction, even kissing him everywhere she could reach, even touching him every which way she knew how...none of it seemed to appease her need to love him.

Desire was starting to scare her. This wasn't like

any book-learning she knew about sex. Gabe wasn't like any man she'd known in any sense. He responded so fiercely to every touch, so explosively to everything she freely gave. The rest of the universe could have dropped dead. There was only him, coming alive, for her, with her. And this bonfire of frustration that kept building, like a clawing ache that burned and burned and wouldn't stop.

"Wait," he whispered.

"No," she whispered back.

But he only lunged away for a moment, to finish stripping off the rest of his clothes. On his way back down to her, he grabbed something from his jeans pocket. Protection.

She saw the condom and felt a sudden clutching. Maybe it wasn't conscious in her mind, but her heart knew him as the one man she'd want to father her babies. Yet a second perception followed that one. There was no objection she could make, nothing she could say, because she knew Gabe. In a fire, in an avalanche, he'd never lose his sense of honor and responsibility, and protecting a woman was irreversibly part of who he was.

He took care of it. And then he took care of her.

Her intent was to love him, but Gabe knew a great deal more about the specifics of such torture than she did. A finger probed, a caress to see if she was wet and ready, a teasing promise of what was to come. She tugged his face down for another kiss, twisted her legs around him to let him know she wasn't interested in this teasing. He could cut it out or die.

There was a wicked smile in his eyes as he shifted closer, but from the moment he began penetration, that smile disappeared. The bones in his face seemed to tighten, and his eyes shone with a glowing raw look of caring and longing. He was in no mood to play. Neither was she. He filled her, slowly yet urgently, making her aware of how empty she'd been without him, making her aware of what belonging to him, with him, meant.

"I love you," she whispered. The words slipped out again, so naturally, so helplessly. That first thrust bound them together, but the crescendo of speed and rhythm that followed seemed to inflame the soul-bond between them. With Gabe, she felt free, to be wild, to be honest, to be herself, as if there were nothing she needed to hold back. Confessing her love was an irrevocable part of that. If she could give him any gift, it was to feel that same freedom with her.

He seemed to. His skin turned slick and slippery, golden in the distant light. So did hers, glowing with radiance and heat. If he'd known pleasure before, there was wonder in his eyes now, a wonder that spilled over into his kisses, poured through his caresses. They began a galloping, dizzy ride that neither of them wanted to end, a joyful test of how long they could tease fate with this speed and this exquisite burning need.

Something happened. Rebecca didn't first recognize what could possibly be wrong. There was just a flash-burst of an instant when that galloping pace suddenly faltered; something changed in Gabe's expression, and he seemed to stop breathing.

He knew before she did that the condom had broken.

Eleven

Gabe either couldn't or didn't stop. Rebecca never considered trying. The passion peaking between them was about more than a roller-coaster ride toward physical satisfaction. It was about cleaving. For her, everything about making love with him was right, her emotions inflamed and aroused by the freedom she felt for Gabe. Love drove her, a gift too vulnerable not to share. He'd touched her soul, and inside her was a boiling-over need to touch him the same way.

Afterward, the feeling of intimacy with him was just as powerful. It took forever for her heartbeat to stop racing. His, too. Somehow she felt even more irrevocably part of him than before. Gabe shifted to her side, yet still cuddled her close. His face, his eyes, the cords in his neck, his disheveled hair…she couldn't stop looking, couldn't stop touching him. And he stroked her back, touched her, kissed her, as if he'd found the same wonder she had in making love together.

For a long time, they lingered like that, sharing a pillow, not talking at all except with their eyes. Eventually, though, he murmured that he needed to get up. He was only in the bathroom for a few minutes. When he came back, he switched off the nuisance television set, flipped off the light and climbed back in bed with her.

But something drastic had changed in those few moments. Except for a ribbon of light sneaking through a slit in the curtains, the room was suddenly as dark as a cave. She couldn't see his eyes, his expression. When he slid under the blankets with her again, she understood he was staying the night, that, Gabe being Gabe—no matter what other emotions he felt—was not the kind of man to have sex with a woman and take a powder.

But his skin was cool instead of warm. And where he'd been relaxed, his muscles and long limbs were suddenly tense and unnaturally still.

Instants before, Rebecca had been powerfully ready to sleep. No more. Her pulse picked up an uneasy beat, thready, broody, worried. She wasn't sure what to say or do; she only sensed that Gabe was distancing himself from her at the speed of light.

And then she felt his fingertips, brushing a strand of hair from her forehead. And his voice was quieter than silence. "I should have stopped, Rebecca. It was my fault."

She squeezed her eyes closed, thinking that she should have realized the broken condom was on his mind, thinking that she needed to be infinitely careful how she responded...or risk everything this night had meant to her, to them. "I don't think *fault* is a fair word. No one was careless. Neither of us could have anticipated ending up on the wrong end of the statistical odds for the chances of one breaking.''

"Yeah, well...the point is—if you end up pregnant, I expect you to tell me. I don't want you to think or worry that it's your problem. It's ours. There's no question about my standing by you, shorty.''

Hurt lanced through her. Responsibility, duty, honor. She knew they were indelibly part of Gabe, but that wasn't what she wanted from him now. It wasn't what she hoped he felt for her.

"I know you have strong feelings about not wanting babies, not wanting a family," she said softly.

"Yeah. Which makes me ten times more at fault.''

"Come on, Gabe. The condom just broke. Neither of us asked for that—''

"There's always a risk of failure with any kind of protection. And for that reason alone, I never made love with a woman unless we were both comfortable with the same set of rules. You were revved up after one hell of a traumatic day, the adrenaline still pumping, your fear level still high. I understood you wanted to be held. You weren't really asking to make love.''

"I very much wanted to make love," she told him swiftly, but right then it seemed she couldn't have sold him his own reflection with a mirror.

"Making love was taking advantage of you, Red. I know what danger is like, what it does to the blood, to your thinking. You didn't, and couldn't possibly, know those things. Maybe you wanted to make love, but you could still regret it like hell in the morning.''

"I won't regret it. I love you, Gabe,'' she said softly, fiercely.

He didn't fall silent for long, but faster than a strike of lightning, she could feel every muscle in his body tense up. "I'm not saying you don't feel love. Or that you're not being honest. But I've never lied to you, shorty, and I wouldn't insult you by doing it now. I don't put the same value on that word *love* that you do.''

She swallowed. Hard. "Devereax?''

"What?''

"I'm not sure how you would define risk. But I can tell you how I do. My dad used to say that you should never play a game that you can't afford to lose. I always saw life differently. I can't see playing any game where the stakes aren't worth winning.''

"You've won some dangerous first prizes as a risk-taker—'' he turned his head "—but it's not relevant in this case, because love is no game to you.''

"No. It isn't. And I know you don't want to hear this, but if I were shopping for a dad for a baby...I'd pick you.''

Again, he tensed. "Then you don't know me worth beans, Rebecca.''

"Yeah, I think I do, but that isn't why I brought the subject up.'' She said gently, firmly, "I need you to know that I wouldn't have trapped you. I wouldn't have done that to any man, much less one I loved. You know how much I want a baby. You know I want a family. But if I wasn't prepared with birth control, it was because I didn't know we were going to make love. I would never have tried to corner you into going against your heart, knowing how you felt about wedding rings and families.''

His eyes found hers in the darkness. ''I believe you. You always were honest to a fault, Red. But what you said was also right—you *didn't* know we were going to make love—which makes me responsible for what happened. I want you to say it aloud, that you'll tell me if you turn up pregnant. I want a promise that you won't try to keep it a secret.''

''It was only the one time. And the chances aren't that likely.'' She knew that was a mile distant from the promise he was asking for, but her heart balked at making a vow she wasn't positive she could keep. She needed more time to think. ''I want to tell you something else.''

''What?''

''I wasn't asking for anything by telling you that I loved you. It wasn't meant to be a rope around your neck or a ring through your nose.'' He'd been tense long enough, she thought. ''I'll love you if I damn well want to, Devereax.'' She shifted on top of him, settled her full weight on his chest and kissed him, slowly and awkwardly and thoroughly. He took his punishment like a man, she noticed. He showed forbearance, patience, courage. He also aroused faster than a firecracker, but, poor baby, he couldn't help that.

"You don't like being loved, cutie?"

He sighed loudly. "God, you're trouble. I swear I knew it the first time I laid eyes on y—"

"You have any more condoms in your jeans pocket?"

"None that I wouldn't be terrified to use," he said dryly.

"Hmm... Well, we could get creative." She kissed his chin. Then aimed for his throat. "You might have to help me think up some ways to get creative. I'm outstanding at research, but pretty much all the research I've done is related to writing mysteries and gruesome murders. A chapter never seemed to come up about seducing men, but you won't believe how fast I learn. Honest. You'll be impressed."

"Has there ever been a time in your life when you didn't invite trouble?"

"Now, now, this is good trouble. It doesn't hurt to be loved. It's not scary. Nothing terrible is going to happen to you. When's the last time you let someone take care of you?"

"I'm a grown man. I can take care of myself."

"That's how much you know, cutie." Since his throat was so convenient, she took a bite out of it. "Everyone needs taking care of sometimes. Now close your eyes and suffer through this. Just practice.

Write it off as a lesson. Just see if you can survive being loved without panicking, huh?''

"Becca," he said…and then nothing else.

She was all through giving him any further chances to talk.

The waiting area for Rebecca's plane was already crowded with tourists carrying luggage and souvenirs. Her flight left at three. She could certainly have taken a taxi alone to the airport, but Gabe had insisted on driving her. She suspected he wanted to make damn sure she was headed home and safe on that plane.

Gabe set her carry-on tote out of harm's way while they were waiting. The scene at the airport was exactly the same as the day she'd arrived. The same blazing Las Vegas sun poured through the windows; the passengers bubbled off the planes with that hot-to-gamble look in their eyes. Exotic posters showing floor shows and casinos lined the walls, and slot machines clattered and rattled from every direction. Her Mickey Mouse sweatshirt was a little more wrinkled on the return trip, but it was exactly what she'd worn that first day, too.

Yet nothing was the same. The difference between now and just a few days ago hit her like a sudden, engulfing wave.

The whole problem with her brother wasn't over. But it nearly was. And once Jake was cleared of the murder charge, the Fortune family would have no further immediate reason to employ Gabe. His job for them was over...which meant that his reason to be connected with her was over, too.

Her heart started thudding, not with anxiety, but just with a building, welling ache. That separation didn't have to be—if Gabe wanted to pursue a personal relationship. If he felt love, as she did. If he even noticed the unique and wondrous specialness they brought each other.

The minute Gabe spotted airport personnel headed for the tarmac, he started jingling the change in his pocket. Typically, his shirt was button-down crisp compared to her floppy sweatshirt, his hair neatly brushed while hers was a sleepy mop of curls. She'd seen him mussed. She'd seen him damn near looking like a disaster—a handsome, unforgettably sexy disaster—but only alone, only when he felt free with her, in bed.

He was as put-back-together now as a stranger. The ache in her heart suddenly hurt like a stabbing. The real Gabe, she knew, was a poignantly vulnerable and giving man, but that Gabe was nowhere in sight now.

"You got money, shorty?"

She forced a smile. "I never have money. But I have forty-seven versions of plastic."

"Is your mom meeting your plane in Minneapolis?"

"My car's already parked at the airport, so there's

absolutely no reason for anyone to meet my plane. I'll see my mom when I get home."

He frowned. "You're not getting in until dark. I'd rather someone were meeting you."

"Sheesh, Devereax. I know you can't change all that sexist overprotective behavior all at once, but I swear, you need a massive retraining course."

It was like expecting a duck to care if it rained. The insult flew right over his head. "You've been through a lot in the last few days."

"Yeah, I have. But so have you."

They called her flight. She bent down to grab her tote and purse. When she straightened up, Gabe yanked his hands out of his pockets and grabbed her shoulders. She saw his eyes just before he ducked down to claim her mouth.

The kiss was lethal. Vintage Devereax. Hot, swift, thorough, less than respectable, a wanton and intoxicating invitation to mayhem and madness...but when the devil got around to lifting his head, she saw it again. The goodbye in his eyes.

It hurt a thousand times more than the feel of Wayne Pott's switchblade directly on her throat. She had to swallow thickly before she could even try speaking again.

"When's your flight home?" she asked him.

"Haven't arranged it yet. Won't even try for at least another day. I want to talk with the cops again, see what happened after their questioning Tracey and

Wayne. There are just some details here that I still want to follow through on."

"And then?"

"And then…I've got a ton of work projects waiting for me at home, in the office. And you'll be going back to your world." The pad of his thumb traced her jawbone. She saw longing in his eyes. She saw love, even if he'd never said the words. But Gabe said nothing about calling her. Nothing about wanting to see her again. And, abruptly, his hand dropped. "You'll let me know if there's a problem?"

Rebecca thought, she should have known he'd bring up the potential-pregnancy problem again. Gabe was ever practical, ever the honorable man.

But if he saw her—and a baby—as a problem, there seemed nothing else to say.

When Rebecca answered the knock on her door, the last person she expected to see was her brother. It'd been five weeks since that long, impossible, unforgettable weekend with Gabe. And three weeks since the murder charges against Jake had been dropped. He was a free man again. But Jake had never made an impromptu visit to her place before.

She promptly threw herself into his arms with a boisterous laugh. "Well, what brings you here, stranger? Come in, come in. You want some coffee or tea?"

"Wouldn't mind some coffee, but I'm guessing

from your appearance that I'm interrupting something..."

Rebecca glanced down, vaguely aware that she'd started out the morning fairly neatly dressed in a black turtleneck and casual flannel skirt. Sometime over the past four hours of writing, she'd lost her shoes and become untucked, and she strongly suspected her hair was standing up in wild tufts. She grinned for her brother. "I get more aerobic exercise writing than some athletes do training for the Olympics. And believe me, I was ready for a break. Make yourself comfortable. Coffee's already made. I'll bring it in."

Minutes later, she carried mugs of a hazelnut brew into her office, where Jake was wandering around. "I think you need a backhoe in here," he teased.

"If you think *this* is messy, you should see it when I haven't cleaned."

"You cleaned in here in the last decade?"

She set down their mugs. Then punched him. When he feigned deep pain, he almost brought tears to her eyes. God, he looked good. Just having the right to look at him, free from those jail bars, was a feast for her eyes—and heart.

Others saw Jake Fortune as a formal, formidable man, Rebecca knew. Very few people had the guts to punch—or tease—him. It took a little sister to get the job done.

He was fifty-four to her thirty-three, but that huge sibling age gap had never troubled either of them.

Gabe had a much brawnier build, but her brother was a respectable six feet, with dark brown hair and a set of green eyes that matched her own. Jake had always been built lean and elegant, but she could see that the time in jail had skinnied him down. It wasn't unusual to see him dressed in a formal navy suit, but even fine tailoring couldn't hide his loss of weight. Or that there was more silver than brown in his hair now.

Her brother had always been a controlled and contained man—except with her. But that kind of control was a choice. She'd always known with a sister's instincts that being caged up in a jail was Jake's worst nightmare. Now, though, he was finally free, and she didn't want to remind him of these past terrible weeks.

"Did you come visiting just to tease and give me grief?" She curled up in her desk chair with her hands wrapped around the coffee mug.

"Actually, I had a different reason." He glanced around for a place to sit and, after lifting five pounds of paper and files off a chair, created one. "This private visit is way overdue, sis. I came to thank you personally. I could still be rotting in that jail if it weren't for you."

Rebecca swiftly shook her head. "Gabe did all the investigative work that mattered, Jake. Not me."

"I've seen Devereax. Thanked him, thanked the whole family, personally." Jake had yet to touch his coffee. "God. I still can't believe how the family stood by me through this mess. I'll never take family for granted again—but you were the only one who did something about it, Rebecca. Don't think I don't know it."

She knew her support had helped him emotionally, but the practical help it really took to free him had come entirely from Gabe. Sometimes the spinning events of the past few weeks still made her mind reel.

Gabe had directly involved himself with the police regarding the questioning of Tracey and Wayne. The nefarious twosome had made a living out of lying, but the cops had grilled them separately, and both had been in such a hustle to cover their behinds that they ended up cooking their own geese. Gabe had followed up on the discrepancies in their tale-telling. The result was that they'd both been charged with conspiracy to commit murder, and Tracey had additionally been charged with murder in the first degree.

Not only was Jake free, but his name had been cleared, and that had mattered desperately to Rebecca. Freedom was more than being loose. Her brother needed the right to hold his head up, needed his pride back. And, thanks to Gabe, he had that.

"You know, there turned out to be a fitting irony in that whole mess," she said thoughtfully. "Tracey and Monica were two of a kind. Neither could define *ethics* with a dictionary. Both were manipulative and greedy, not above blackmail or stealing or any other criminal activity. I'm not saying it's right that Monica was murdered. But those two running into each other was like a witch finding her familiar.''

Jake nodded. ''Almost eerie, those two black cats crossing paths in the night. Monica threatening Tracey, to keep the secret quiet about her kidnapping our brother decades ago. Who would have thought that Tracey would investigate Monica and discover she'd so conveniently adopted Brandon just after the twin disappeared. And only someone with that devious mind would make the connection and confront Monica. Tracey saw murder as a way to keep *her* secrets, so she could capitalize on a financial scam.'' Abruptly he looked weary. ''Maybe it's a twist of irony that those two were immoral predators exactly the same way...but I think a lot of grief could have been saved over the years, if the Fortune family hadn't tried to hide so many secrets.''

''Including yours?'' Rebecca asked gently. ''How are you and Erica doing after all this? I know the girls have stood by you, but how are things with Adam?'' She'd never been close to Erica, his wife. But Adam was his only son, and more Rebecca's age—the two growing up together had been thick as thieves—and she knew father and son had been emotionally estranged.

Jake admitted frankly, ''It's going really good, though I still have a lot of fences to mend with my family. I made a lot of mistakes, took a lot of wrong turns.'' He hesitated. ''You know...the reason I got involved with Monica to begin with was because she was blackmailing me. I never did know how she found out that my genetic father wasn't Ben Fortune. But I responded with panic. I thought I'd lose everything—my wife, my work, my whole life—if it came out that I wasn't in the direct bloodline to be a Fortune heir. It wasn't only about losing *money*, Rebecca. Or about a fear of losing money. It was about being afraid I would lose my whole life.''

He lurched out of the chair, and started restlessly pacing around her cramped office. "That was part of what was so unbearable about being charged with murder. I'd been drinking. I *did* go to confront Monica. I *was* angry. But I had no motivation on earth to kill her. I know it looked that way—but I'd already accepted that the truth about my background needed to come out. I'd had it with living a lie. I'd come to the conclusion that I wouldn't, couldn't, live that way anymore. Only I had no way to make anyone believe that.''

"I'm afraid the truth doesn't always show up as evidence in a court of law," Rebecca murmured, thinking of Gabe and all the times they'd bickered about the validity of facts versus intuition. Harshly she slammed her mind's door on that train of thought, though. Even a mention of Gabe induced a fierce, aching pain for which there seemed no salve...and this was no time to deal with that, not with her brother here. "Jake, you still didn't say how your wife and son are handling all the 'real truth' that's come out.''

"They're okay. More than okay. Adam…he never gave a damn who I was. It was my being dishonest and hiding things that nearly destroyed our relationship. Afraid he's a better and more ethical man than his dad."

"I think you're a pretty good guy yourself, bro," Rebecca said. "Anyone can lose their way and make mistakes."

"Yeah, well, I'm afraid I did both, big-time. As far as Erica…we're back together. And I'll be damned if I don't think we might have a shot at one hell of a marriage. The woman loves me."

"This is a shock to you?" Rebecca teased gently.

"I thought she loved the Fortune heir. I thought she loved all the trappings, the money, the position." Jake shook his head. "I was always trying to be the man I thought she wanted. We wasted a hell of a lot of years not being honest with each other…."

The ring of a telephone interrupted them. Both the phone and the answering machine were buried on a far table, under some pillows and papers and a needlework project. Her brother would never have picked up her telephone, even assuming he could pin down its location, but his eyebrows raised in a silent query when she didn't immediately answer it.

Rebecca had no intention of answering it, but she braced herself, going as stiff as a fireplace poker, at the sound of the first ring. The answering machine was programmed to kick in after two.

Gabe's voice came on. Slow, quiet, sexy-husky,

and painfully familiar. "One of these times I'm going to find you in, shorty. Rebecca...I *need* to talk to you."

That was the whole message, but it was enough to rivet Jake's attention. He studied her face with an older brother's shrewd eyes. "You knew who it was, didn't you? Why didn't you pick up the phone?" he asked her.

"Because you're here, and I don't get a chance to talk with you very often, and I can easily call him back another time."

"You're the worst liar I ever met, sis. What's wrong? Was that Gabe? I couldn't recognize the voice, because it was so muffled with all the junk piled on top of the machine—"

"Nothing's wrong. Absolutely everything's fine," she assured him cheerfully, and quickly turned the conversation back to family business. Jake stayed another half hour. When he had to leave, she walked him to the door, thinking that he'd forgotten about that phone call. But he hugged her before he left.

He also gently cocked up her chin to deliver a brotherly mini lecture. "If you need help, any kind, I'd be really ticked if you don't give me the chance to come through for you. The whole family stood by me through this mess, but you, squirt, were my main line to sanity. I'd be there for you so fast it'd make your head spin, and no questions asked."

"Thanks, sweetie." She knew her brother meant the offer, but there were certain problems that a woman simply had to face alone. When Jake was gone, she pressed a hand on her abdomen.

The container for the pregnancy test was in the bathroom. She'd known the results for three days.

She walked back into her office, switched on the computer and pulled up the chapter she'd been working on. Work had been her salvation for weeks now. Normally her mind blocked out everything else when she was writing, and before her brother's visit, she'd left a hero hanging in terrible danger. She needed to fix the crisis and save him, yet minutes ticked by. The cursor kept blinking, but no words would come.

Right next to the computer, she kept her Abe Lincoln teddy bear with the sad hound-dog eyes. He'd been her pal on bad writing days for years now. She picked him up and snuggled him, and when that didn't work, she fingered the talisman charm bracelet on her wrist. Both had always been symbols of comfort for her.

Neither worked worth spit today. She wrapped her arms around her legs and closed her eyes. Gabe had been trying to contact her for a week now. Using the answering machine to dodge him was immature and stupid and dishonest…but, temporarily, Rebecca just didn't feel ready to talk with him.

He could have called weeks before this. He hadn't, and his long silence hurt like a wound. Rebecca was no fan of logic, but Gabe certainly was. The sudden calls had an all-too-logical reason. Enough time had now passed for her to know if she'd missed a period or could be pregnant.

Weeks ago, as of that one long, unforgettable night together, she'd decided not to tell him if she was carrying a baby. He had always made his feelings about not wanting a child or family clear. Gabe was so damned honorable and old-fashioned that she had no doubt he'd offer a ring if he believed her pregnant. Rebecca couldn't imagine a worse disaster. No love could grow where a partner felt trapped, and she was afraid his feelings of resentment would end up destroying them both.

If Gabe had called her before, she might have believed they had a chance. Love might have built for him, from what they had already started. But now was simply too late. It seemed logically obvious that only his sense of honor and responsibility motivated his calls at this point. She could, she knew damn well, fall into bed with him again. She could, she was afraid, fall into any relationship he was willing to consider. Her pride had never stopped her picking up the phone.

But loving him did.

She opened her eyes and stared blindly at the spring buds out the window. She'd never met a man who needed love more than Gabe. Relationships based on duty or responsibility were all he seemed to believe in. It would take the right woman to give him a whomp upside the head. The right woman would make him feel free—free to let loose that huge, vulnerable tenderness inside him, free to discover that real love wasn't a cage, but an opening-up of choices and possibilities. The right woman could make a giant and wonderful difference in his life.

But it didn't seem to be her. Tears stung and burned her eyes, but she squeezed them back, unshed. Crying was no solace. Gabe had teased her dozens of times about being unrealistic, but Rebecca saw no choice but to face this reality. She hadn't been able to break Gabe out of his prison. Love—or her brand of love—either wasn't right or wasn't enough. Not for him.

She'd tasted hardship before. She'd known loss. She knew all the flavors of loneliness. But nothing in her life had ever ached like knowing she'd lost him.

Twelve

When her secretary tracked her down in the lab,
Kate Fortune was just finishing a meeting with two
of her chemists. Her mood was exhilarated. The Secret Youth Formula was her newest and most am-
bitious product, yet problems and sabotage—more of
Monica's doing—had crippled her new baby from
the start. Finally those problems had been resolved,
and the last studies and tests completed successfully.
Her brainchild was almost ready to take wing. When
her secretary delivered the message that Gabe Devereax was in the downstairs lobby, she was delighted
to have the break.

She strode into the lobby with both her hands out-
stretched to take his in greeting. "Well, if this isn't
a surprise! I can't believe you didn't come right up.
You should have known you didn't need to stand on
any ceremony with me."

"I wasn't sure if it was still kosher protocol to
wander upstairs, now that I'm no longer in your employ."

"Bosh on protocol. I've missed you, Gabe."

He chuckled. "Well, that's a relief. There was a
good chance you'd feel the opposite. The only times

I was around, you were having trouble with sabotage or kidnapping or murder. I had a bad feeling you might associate being around me with the wrong kind of excitement.''

Kate heard the humor in his voice and saw his familiar dry smile. But something was seriously different in his appearance, his manner, his eyes. Trying to figure it out, she steered him toward her private elevator and kept an easy conversation going. "I'm afraid excitement comes with responsibility for a financial empire. I admit I wouldn't mind a nice long stretch with no trouble—it does seem like we've had our share in recent times. But I've missed talking with you, far beyond all the investigative work you've done for us. And so has Sterling.''

Kate could hear her voice automatically softening when she mentioned the longtime Fortune attorney and friend. Gabe had spent as much time with Sterling Foster as with her. One of these days, she probably needed to get around to telling the family exactly how deeply her feelings for Sterling went. Now though, she ushered Gabe upstairs and into her private office.

"You haven't said why you stopped. You were never much for idle chitchat, Gabe, but I don't know what business we could have. I'm pretty sure our check to you didn't bounce," she said, deadpan.

Again, she won a grin, but it didn't linger more than a slash of a second. "Uh, no. Your check spent fine. So did the generous bonus, Kate.''

"It wasn't generous. I'm an extremely smart woman, dear. I never give money away for nothing. You earned every penny."

He ignored the praise, and though he entered the office, she couldn't get him to take a chair. He stood as stiff as a poker and jammed his hands in his pockets. "This visit is about a personal matter. I want to talk to you about your daughter."

"Hmm. Somehow I don't think you mean Lindsay." Thoughtfully Kate ambled over to the sterling-silver tea set on the credenza. "Would you like some coffee? Tea? Something stronger?"

"You may not feel like offering me anything when I tell you what I'm here for, Kate."

"My, that sounds ominous." Privately she mused that it sounded far more interesting than ominous. The last time they talked, she'd sensed chemistry building between Gabe and her youngest daughter. Kate had thought a great deal about that since. Still, as tactfully—and relentlessly—as she'd tried to worm information out of her daughter, Rebecca had revealed precisely nothing.

Gabe's appearance, though, told her a great deal. It took a minute before she realized what was so different about his looks. During all the months he'd done investigative work for the Fortunes, Kate had never seen his appearance less than neat, contained, professional. Gabe simply gave away nothing about himself with his clothes or his expression. He not only looked like, but had proved to be, a brick in a crisis.

But he hadn't had a haircut in a month, she noticed now. His hair was shaggy; his boots were scuffed; his rugged face looked thinner and more gaunt. If he hadn't been in a fight, he appeared to be looking for one. His shoulder muscles were bunched and braced, and his whole posture was edgy.

Typically, he didn't beat around the bush. "I've been trying to reach your daughter for three weeks now. If I call, she's ducking me with an answering machine. If I show up, she's either not there or bolted up tight behind a locked door."

"Hmm..." Shrewd eyes studied him again. "Well, Rebecca has been known to hole up like a hermit when she's writing, Gabe. But if you're asking for my help in reaching her—"

"Hell, no. That's not your problem. It's mine." Gabe scrubbed a hand over his face. "Kate, you may kick my behind from here to Siberia when you hear what I have to say. There's no way· you're going to like it. But the alternative was to shut up and put you in a position where you'd worry. I've worked too damn close with you over these last months. It seemed to me that you've had enough children to worry about because of secrets that were kept from you."

"This is getting more fascinating by the minute," Kate murmured, but she doubted he heard her, doubted he would hear anything anyone said right then. Clearly too wired to sit, he stood there, bristling with more virile, potent, electric energy than an imminent crack of lightning. "You know, I'm inclined to pour a sherry, even if it is only four in the afternoon—"

"I intend to kidnap your daughter, Kate."

"Ah."

"Since she's been avoiding me like I have an infectious disease, I'm not sure she'll go with me willingly. Which is why I may have to go the kidnapping route."

Those dark eyes met hers squarely—full of defiance, full of defensiveness, full of fire. He seemed to expect her to knock his block off, which Kate technically wouldn't mind doing. Even at seventy-one, she'd never lost her love for a challenging fight—and she'd metaphorically TKOed more than one adversary who mistakenly assumed that a woman would fold near real trouble.

Regrettably, though, she couldn't give Gabe what he seemed to badly want. "Do you, um, have any particular location in mind as far as this kidnapping?"

"No. Haven't got that down yet. But I'm thinking along the lines of a desert island with no phones and no way out. In no way am I asking your permission, Kate. I can imagine what you're thinking. The only reason I'm telling you is that if—and when—your daughter suddenly disappears, I couldn't have you worrying she was dead or injured or some terrible thing had happened to her. She'll be with me.''

"This is quite a bomb to drop in a mother's lap. I want you to know that I'm shocked and appalled," Kate said primly, and then paused. "If you can't find an island deserted enough, I could put the family yacht at your disposal."

"I... Come again?''

"I just offered you the use of the family yacht. Or would one of the planes be more helpful?''

Gabe didn't answer. He couldn't have looked more bewildered if an elephant had walked into the room. Kate's opinion that he really hadn't heard a word she said before this was confirmed. Fascinating, how gut-sure he'd been that she'd be opposed to his involvement with Rebecca.

He'd clearly expected to face a bullet from her.

Kate smoothly poured him a glass of sherry instead. It was an awfully sissy drink for Mr. Devereax, but she kept no hard spirits in the office. A little bolster would surely help. He looked as if he were suffering from shock.

More relevant, he was unlikely to talk unless he was more relaxed. And Kate certainly had no intention of letting him leave until she'd heard a great deal more about Gabe and her daughter than she'd heard so far.

Gabe noted that all the maples were leafing out in Rebecca's neighborhood. Daffodils and tulips peeked from flower beds. The grass had already turned that lush velvet green unique to spring.

Spring might be the season for love, but the rest of the omens weren't good. Ponderous black clouds were roiling in from the west, turning the afternoon darker than gloom. When Gabe pulled into Rebecca's driveway, the streets were deserted. There were no kids on swing sets or bikes anywhere, no ambling walkers, no moms pushing strollers. Lightning striped the sky. Thunder cracked loud enough to smack the eardrums.

Gabe opened the door of his Morgan, and using both hands, lifted his left leg outside the car. The Velcro cast fit the limb from knee to ankle. The cast made wearing a shoe on that foot impossible, and mobility was additionally tough because of the tan canvas sling holding his left arm close to his chest. Slowly, awkwardly, he stepped out. Slowly, awkwardly, he managed to get the crutch out and installed under his armpit.

A curtain stirred in Rebecca's front window.

Gabe made a grimace of pain. And stopped for a moment to rub his right temple hard—the one with the butterfly bandage.

Big, fat spatters of rain started to splash down. Cold rain. His sweatshirt wouldn't stay dry long, and his jeans had had to be cut to accommodate the Velcro cast. The spattering drips almost immediately turned into a steady driving rain. Still, there was no way he could hustle, when the fastest he could move was a hobble.

If he turned into a duck in the deluge—or got hit by lightning—there was no way he wanted to move fast, anyway.

Her front door was a long twenty feet away. Long enough for any chance passerby to see what pitiful shape he was in. Long enough for Gabe to mentally replay parts of the strange conversation he'd had with Kate Fortune in her office.

Considering that he came from the wrong side of the tracks, had never had an ounce of education or polish—and for damn sure had never been near an Armani suit—Gabe still wasn't sure why Kate hadn't raised hell over his involvement with her daughter. She hadn't even asked if marriage was on his mind.

Instead, she'd poured him a glass of sickly-sweet cream sherry and rambled down a side conversational track. Over the past two years, her whole family had been thrown into chaos, she'd told him. "Every one of my children has suffered through some kind of serious personal crisis. We also had sabotage and financial problems affecting the business—which you know well, Gabe. Somehow, though, each of my children has grown and ended up stronger, happier, closer. With one exception."

"Rebecca," Gabe had guessed.

"Yes. Rebecca." Kate had poured herself a crystal glass of that sherry, but she never had gotten around to taking a sip from it. "I could help all my children, except for her. Others see us as totally unlike because Rebecca doesn't have my head for business. That's poppycock. She's extremely bright, just in a different way from me, and in personality I'm afraid we're two peas in a pod. She's never done one thing by anyone else's rules, and nothing sways her when she's determined. I want to see her happy. I want to see her settled. I want to see her with the houseful of children she wants. But of all the men who've come knocking on her door, there hasn't been one, not one, who made her nervous. Until you.''

Nervous.

Gabe took another hobbling step toward Rebecca's front door, thinking that the word *nervous* had been stuck in his mind for days now. Damned if he knew what Kate Fortune was trying to tell him. Damned if he knew if *nervous* meant something good—or something worrisome—when it came to Rebecca's feelings for him.

No matter what the consequences, he'd discovered that he couldn't wait any longer to find out.

Weeks ago, when Jake was freed, Gabe had been relieved that job was over, relieved that stacks of work kept him busy, relieved to have space away from Rebecca. As always, he'd been thrilled with his solitude and freedom.

Then came the flulike symptoms. An emptiness, gnawing at his gut. A sick-sad malaise that he couldn't shake. A feeling of loss so huge that he couldn't eat, couldn't sleep. The fever was all for her, but there seemed no recovery from the symptoms.

He forced himself to remember—a ton of times—all the memories of his parents fighting, sniping and biting at each other, turning whatever might have been love into a house of tension and silent bitterness. Every wildly-in-love couple seemed to rant and rave about "love" in the beginning. It never lasted.

His whole life, Gabe had been determined to be a realist. Love was real; it just had no endurance factor. If you never bought into the fairy tale, you never had to go through the pain of disillusionment. If you made yourself self-sufficient, you never had to need anyone else.

At some point, when he was suffering the worst symptoms of that flu, Gabe had the oddest realization. The memories of all those couples fighting and destroying each other had mightily motivated his loner philosophy. But he'd fought with Rebecca from the start. Had, in fact, loved their fights and sparring matches.

He wanted the right to fight with her. Until they were both a hundred and ten. Maybe longer.

More disastrous emotional conclusions had followed that one. Gabe knew—he *knew*—what dangerous trouble that redhead could get into. No one else did. She had family up the wazoo—they all loved her—but no one seemed to have any influential power over her behavior. For damn sure, no one was keeping her safe.

Somebody on this planet had to believe in white knights. Somebody had to believe in the good of man, and that good won over evil, and that nothing would hurt you if you just did what was right.

Gabe didn't give a particular damn about anyone else on the planet. Just her. He wanted *her* to have the freedom to believe in those things. But if that was going to happen, someone had to protect her, subtly and with care. Someone who understood how vulnerable, how special, how wonderful, she was. Someone who was strong enough to sit on her from time to time. Someone who'd talk back. Who'd love back. Someone who understood that Rebecca would never thrive with repressive jail bars around her, limiting what she did...but that somebody *really* needed to be standing by her.

And that was when it occurred to Gabe that he didn't want anyone standing by her side...except him.

He loved that woman.

Loved her so bad he ached with it. And then, one night, he wakened from a nightmare, picturing Rebecca with a child in her belly. His child. The picture hit him with the impact of a nuclear warhead, with a longing to be a father that he hadn't even known he had. Not a father like his own...but a father his own way. A family his own way.

The nightmare aspect of the dream—the cold sweat he woke up with—came from knowing she'd never tell him if she was pregnant. It should have been obvious before this. Shorty had never made a secret of the fact that she wanted all or nothing—love, rings, the picket fence, the whole nine yards. No way that damn woman would remotely consider settling for less. Which meant that, unless she believed that whole corny future was a possibility, Red would never pick up a phone to call him. Not for a baby. Not for any other reason, either.

The curtain stirred in her front window again. This time it parted several inches.

Gabe winced in pain. He hobbled another agonizing couple of feet toward the porch, slowly, ignoring the rain slithering down his neck, when—miracle of miracles—her front door was suddenly hurled open.

"Gabe! I saw movement from my window, even saw your bent head coming up the walk, but I didn't realize it was you at first! My Lord! What on earth happened to you?"

"A little accident," he confessed. For a moment, he almost forgot to look pitiful. He just wanted to inhale the sight of her. He didn't see any of that "nervousness" her mother seemed to think was so critically important…but one problem at a time. Lifting a ton of worry off his head, he saw her ragged-hemmed white sweatshirt, her hair wisping all over the place, her bare feet—and a wonderful look of panic and concern in her eyes.

"A *little* accident? Good grief, Gabe—"

"I could use some help, shorty, and that's the truth." As soon as he reached the overhang of her porch, he leaned hard on the crutch. "I need a place to recover, to just hole up for a bit of rest time…and

I've got the place. But I'd have a real hard time driving there myself, much less carrying groceries and supplies inside. Once I set up, I'll be fine alone. But if you could spare an afternoon..." He took a breath. "I need you, Red."

His voice sounded strange, harsh and curt, not at all how he'd intended those words to come out. But he'd never admitted to needing anyone before, and it came hard. He was afraid she'd think he was lying through his teeth, and it was true that there were some details that included some reprehensible fibs. But the part about needing her was the truest thing he'd ever said.

She searched his eyes. Only for a second or two. But he could have sworn she responded instantly, intuitively, to the honesty in his. "I need to shut off my computer and grab a purse," she said swiftly.

"And shoes, shorty."

"To hell with shoes."

She came back out wearing shoes, though, and, moving faster than a speeding bullet, she bullied and mothered him into the passenger side of the Morgan. The plan was for her to drive, help him get set up, take the car and come pick him up in a week. Gabe knew damn well it was a hokey, illogical plan, but perhaps it was a good thing Rebecca was an idealistic, imaginative writer. She seemed to accept it wholesale.

Gabe had a few more things he needed her to accept wholesale to get any of this to work. He gave her directions. An hour north of the bustling Minneapolis freeways, they turned onto country roads. Rebecca paid more attention to stealing glances at his injuries—and his face—than the geography.

When they stopped at a grocery store, though, she turned into an army general. She allowed him to come in, but picked and chose all the groceries, ignoring any input from him, and hoisted all the grocery bags herself. When he gave her no grief and responded with meek obedience, she charged over and laid a palm on his brow. "Are you sure you're not running a fever?"

"You think I'm running a fever because I'm being nice?"

"You've never obeyed me before, cutie. No leopard changes its spots that fast. Of course, there could be another reason why you're not yourself. You're probably taking a lot of pain meds?"

"Hmm..." he said. There were a lot of complicated directions to give her after that. Eventually the blacktop country road twisted and turned into a gravel lane. The lane led through a roller coaster of woods and meadows, typical of Minnesota's backwoods. Gabe directed her through enough misguided turns and backturns to confuse a geographer with a compass.

They pulled up in a grassy driveway a half hour later. Rebecca stepped out first, her hands on her hips, and looked the whole scene over. The cedar cabin was multilevel, built on a hillside. Virgin woods sheltered the back in cool shade. The front had glass doors, leading onto a deck, with a view of a rambling silver creek gurgling and splashing diamonds at the base of the hill.

"It's gorgeous, Gabe. You rented this?"

"Yeah, for a week."

"Well, I can't think of a better place on earth to rest and relax, but it's awfully secluded. I didn't even see another house or cabin for at least a half mile back."

She carried in the groceries, ordering him to "just rest" while she looked around inside. He waited, tension knotting in his stomach like a thousand drunk butterflies, when she disappeared. He knew what she'd see. Inside were hardwood floors and a fieldstone hearth, stacked with firewood, the furniture all russets and browns. The kitchen was rustic, with a gnarled pine table. There was only one bedroom—a maestro-size room with a skylight, overlooking the view, with a king-size bed and built-in drawers. Nothing in the house was fancy, but the bathroom had a redwood sauna.

When Rebecca came back out, her hands were on her hips again. "It's beautiful. An absolutely idyllic retreat. But no telephone?"

"Nope, no phone."

"No phone and no neighbors. What if you fall? What if you can't get around with all these steps and need some help?" She tapped her foot. "I'm not sure about leaving you here alone."

"I've coped alone my whole life, shorty."

"You weren't hurt before."

"Not like I'm hurting now," he agreed. "Rebecca?"

She turned her head. He opened his palm to show her the car keys, and then, while she was watching, hurled them in the air. As far as touchdown passes went, this one was pretty good. The keys landed with a plop and a splash in the creek.

Rebecca's jaw fell open. "I don't believe I just watched you do that! Have you lost your mind? What on earth are you thinking of? Without the car keys, neither of us have any way to get out of here—"

While she was still watching, he tossed the crutch on the grass. After peeling off the itchy butterfly bandage on his temple, he yanked off the arm sling, then bent down to undo all the fastenings on the Velcro cast.

It took a good three minutes before he could stand up straight again. Three minutes. To risk his heart— a heart he'd never risked, not for anyone or anything—and hurl it at her feet. His heart couldn't have beaten any harder if he was in the middle of a nightmare.

She hadn't moved. Hadn't budged. Hadn't shifted her eyes from his for even a second. But it seemed to take a couple of centuries before she got around to saying anything.

Gabe figured there was a damn good chance she was gonna kill him.

Thirteen

Rebecca deliberately, slowly, circled around him. His normally tanned and ruddy complexion looked a little pale, but there wasn't a bruise in sight. Once he peeled off that silly cast, an extremely healthy, hairy calf showed up—with no injury of any kind. Those linebacker's shoulders were flexed tight, certainly indicating no malfunction in the muscle department, and there wasn't a single cut or scrape on his chin or forehead—not even shaving nicks. Possibly she had a certain bias, but personally she thought Gabe could star in an anatomy textbook as a prize male specimen.

The longer she studied him, though, the more he got the wary, edgy look of a cornered cougar.

"You aren't injured," she announced.

"No."

"You weren't in some life-threatening accident."

"I got a mosquito bite last night, putting away the barbecue. But the last time I was near any remotely life-threatening injuries was in Vegas. With you. Rebecca?"

"What?"

"Somehow you don't seem...all that surprised."

"Of course I'm not surprised, Devereax. I know you, for crying out loud. Put you in an alley with six thugs, and I'd feel sorry for the thugs. If there was ever a man born who could take care of himself, it's you. What did you think, that I was buying this rhinestone? That I'd just leap to take off cross-country on a trumped up story about a bunch of pitiful injuries, without asking you a single question? I write fiction, for Pete's sake. I can recognize a contrived plot blindfolded."

Uneasily Gabe cleared his throat. His eyes were on her face now, as relentlessly as the beat of a heart. "But...you came."

"Of course I came. I was worried sick." She immediately corrected herself. "I'm still worried sick. It isn't like you to lie. Something had to be seriously wrong for you to go to all this ridiculous trouble."

"There was. You didn't want to see me. I couldn't even get you to answer the phone. It was pretty damn obvious I had to do something creative to get your attention."

"Well, you certainly did that." She *had* avoided him. Because she hadn't wanted to answer any questions about whether or not she was pregnant until she was ready. But during the incredibly long drive to the cabin, she couldn't help but notice that Gabe had ample time and opportunity to bring up that subject. Yet he hadn't. Maybe foolishly, she had built up courage because that didn't seem to be Gabe's first priority. "So...you wanted to talk to me."

"I did," he muttered. "But I've had about all the conversation I can handle for now."

She was still circling around him, fists still propped on her hips, when he hauled her into his arms. Not taking any chances on her acquiescence, he folded her small, clenched fists around his nape and molded them chest-to-chest. She could feel his sick-scared heartbeat thudding against her sick-scared heartbeat. And then he took a kiss.

She'd been afraid he would kiss her. So afraid. She'd known how easy it would be to sink into Gabe's arms again. The chemistry was so magical, so compelling, that she suspected it might damn well last forever, and she'd only fall more deeply and more hopelessly in love if she was with him.

That first kiss was everything she'd worried about...and more. His mouth settled on hers like the dew on a rose. With infinite slowness, his lips rubbed against hers, as if he were taking a long, tender sip of her. As if she were a drink for a man who'd been dying in the desert, dry on the inside, thirsty for her, only for her.

A wistful spring breeze ruffled the trees. Leaves sprinkled droplets of water on both of them. She could hear water gurgling in the distant stream, smell the briny pines, feel the squish of wet grass through her shoes.

His mouth was softer than moonlight, and his arms were warmer than any sun. The dreams she'd wanted to believe in her whole life seemed real at the moment. Yet she felt so fragile she was scared of breaking.

"Gabe..." Her voice came out thicker than wet sugar. It was the best she could do.

"I know, we need to talk. And I *want* to talk with you, shorty. But right now all I really want is to find out if I can make you nervous."

"Nervous? Why on earth would you want me to be nervous?"

"Damned if I know. But it's important." He scooped her up, wrapping her legs around his waist, facing her as he walked up the steps to the house, kissing her every third step. "We have to work on this, Red. I don't think I can even try to do any more talking until we've got this settled."

"About my being nervous?"

"Yeah. We're headed for the king-size bed in the back bedroom with the skylight. Does that make you nervous?"

"Uh...no. Should it?" The screen door banged behind them. He was still looking at her, still carrying her, still strewing kisses on her nose and jaw, in her hair, anywhere he could reach.

"We're not playing checkers in there," he warned her.

"Somehow I guessed that." His shoulder grazed the dark log paneling in the hall. He was going to be all bruised up if he didn't start looking where he was going.

"This isn't about sex. Just so you know. It's about

needing you. It's about mourning every day of my life that you weren't in it. It's about thinking I was free until I met you, and discovering I was never free. Not to be myself. Not until you. Now does *that* make you nervous?''

"No, Gabe," she whispered.

"I love you. *Love* you, shorty. Like I never loved anyone. Like I never believed I could love anyone, like I never believed I could even feel. Now, for God's sakes, Red, I'm getting desperate here. What the hell does it take to make you nervous?''

Eventually, Rebecca thought, they really needed to get this "nervous" business straightened out.

Just then, her man was a mess. It wasn't like all those things she'd been terribly afraid of suddenly disappeared. But Gabe was so rattled and shook up. He needed handling now.

They'd reached the bedroom, after chasing through the rest of the house at breakneck speed, but he seemed confounded about what to do with her then. He seemed unwilling to let her down. He seemed unwilling to stop kissing her. But they didn't seem to be moving past the threshold, either.

"Gabe," she whispered, "I'm not going anywhere if you let me go."

"I'm not letting you go," he said fiercely, but, most uneasily, he let her feet drop to the floor.

She peeled off his sweatshirt. Kissed him. Then flipped the catch on his jeans and kissed him again. When such wantonly aggressive moves failed to dent the desperate look in his eyes, she slid her hands inside the denim and cupped his tight fanny boldly, possessively. Possibly her fingers were trembling a little too much for her to qualify in the true-seductress category.

But that lost expression on his face slowly changed to something else. And so did the emotion in his eyes. One dark, shaggy eyebrow raised. "I don't think you're nervous at all," he said accusingly.

"I think you'd better be. If you can't recognize when you're in big trouble, cutie, then let me give you a clue or two."

She pushed him. That was all it took to tumble him on the bed. She peeled off everything she had on, first a shoe, then her sweatshirt, then the other shoe, and her underpants skinned down at the same time she yanked off her jeans. A Hudson's Bay blanket draped the king-size bed, the wool fabric scratchy and rough. The blanket couldn't have been a more total erotic, exotic contrast to Gabe.

He was satin. Man-satin. His skin was warm and smooth and supple under her stroking hands. Gabe was so tough, but he melted like butter under a wet, openmouthed woman's kiss. Tenderness took him under every time.

He loved her. She'd heard him say it, inhaled and savored those words she'd never expected to hear, not from him. But now she felt his love in every answering kiss, every volatile response of his body, every look in his eyes. There was yearning and need and an ache of fear in his eyes that she wanted gone. There was a love song in those eyes, about a vulnerable, lost boy who'd sworn to be tough...and about a grown man who was trying to learn not to be.

Driven by instinct, by intuition, by love, she unraveled him...one skein of kisses at a time. There were questions between them that still needed answering, but loving him was an answer, too. Right now, she simply belonged to him, with him. Every fear that she'd lost him poured into her touch. Every dark night, every nightmare under the bed, she expressed with her hands, with her kisses, with the need she laid raw and bare for him. It was no time for secrets, no time to deny what she felt. He was her match, her mate, the only man she'd ever wanted in her life.

A watery late-afternoon sun shone down from the skylight. Slowly that light turned misty, then the gray-silver of dusk. They loved, then loved again. They shared kisses that scalded and kisses that healed, caresses drenched in earthiness and embraces silkened with tenderness. They climbed and re-climbed a ruby red cliff of rapture, seeking to please each other, seeking to give, then give more. Rebecca could have sworn he touched her soul. She had never felt more free with another human being. With all her heart, she hoped the power of love would help him feel the same way.

Afterward, she remembered crashing in his arms,

with her pulse still thudding like thunder. But she was unaware of falling asleep until she woke later.

Groggily she realized that it was full night, now, and the scratchy wool blanket had disappeared. Gabe had pulled a soft sheet over her, and switched on the bedside lamp. He was lying beside her, wide awake, his eyes on her face, on her.

A frown was embedded in his brow. Not a scowl. Just a grave, concentrating expression that Rebecca had seen a dozen times before. She was well aware that Gabe had always depended on himself to handle and solve problems on his own, and all the unanswered questions between them suddenly loomed in her mind.

She reached up to gently smooth that frown from his forehead. She was scared to speak, but more scared not to. Either she trusted him with her heart, or she could hardly ask him to take that same perilous risk. "I'm going to have your baby, Gabe," she said quietly.

She expected wariness. Instead, his eyes seemed to fill with a shimmering, glowing light. "Thank God. If we have a houseful of miniature Devereax, maybe there's a chance of keeping you so busy you won't have time to get in trouble. Except for trouble with me."

She raised up on an elbow, not fooled by the devil's attempt at humor. "This can't be a marriage proposal. The last I knew, you were dead-set against marriage. Families. Babies."

"Yeah, well, falling in love with you forced me to rethink that. I was never against any of those things. I was against making a mistake, and I can't lie to you, shorty—I'm a bad risk. I don't know half as much about trust and love as you do."

"I think you're the best risk I've ever known. I already know you're not going to cut and run if there's trouble."

"You've got that right."

"I already know we're going to fight."

"I figured that out, too. For a long time, I mistakenly associated fighting with automatically hurting someone else. But we've always fought, Red, and for some damn reason I even love going to war with you. I can't swear we'll always agree, but my intention would never be to hurt you. I want you to be strong on your own terms. Those terms don't have to be mine. I love you, Rebecca."

He peppered her face with soft, slow kisses. Kisses filled with promise. Kisses filled with that new, soft light in his eyes. "I'm going to keep doing this until you give me a clear-cut yes," he warned.

"Then you're asking to suffer for a long time, because I'm not about to give you an excuse to stop."

"You gonna be this ruthless after we get married?"

"I plan to be this ruthless for the next fifty, sixty years. You asked for trouble, Devereax. Trust me, I intend to give you plenty."

"I do trust you."

She knew. She could see it in his eyes. And her heart suddenly brimmed to overflowing. "You can have your clear-cut yes," she whispered. "Yes, yes, yes. I used to dream of the right kind of love, Gabe. I never was willing to settle for less, but I never expected to find it. Until you. However..."

"However?"

"However, how the patooties are we ever going to get home if you threw away the car keys?"

"It's possible that I have another set of keys."

"Being a logical, rational man, I would assume so," she teased him.

"Actually, I've recently taken up trusting my instincts and intuition. I know that sounds crazy...." He paused. "Well, no, *you* wouldn't think that was crazy, since you're the one who taught me to trust, shorty, but..."

"But?"

"But there are a few repercussions to behaving impulsively."

"You don't have a second set of car keys?"

"Yeah, I do. At home. But not here."

"Are you trying to tell me we're stuck in this cabin alone together?"

"Yup."

"Really stuck here? Indefinitely?"

"Yup."

"Good," she murmured, and reached over to turn out the light.

Epilogue

Kate was rarely frazzled. She'd been down too many life trails to ever have much throw her. She'd survived a plane crash, threats to her life, sabotage, enemies ceaselessly jealous both of her and of the fortune it had taken a long life to win. She had endured. She knew herself to be strong. Another hurricane was simply water off a duck's back.

But a wedding in the house was something else.

She stood on the balcony, wringing her hands, overlooking the yard. The expansive lakeside estate outside Minneapolis was home, and a mighty far cry from the orphanage where she had grown up. Still, there was no way Kate could make things perfect enough—not today.

She studied the yard, searching for any detail she could have missed. Buckets of camellias lined the white-carpet path for the bride. A summer breeze drifted from the lake, ruffling leaves, carrying the whispered perfume of flowers in the air. Guests were already congregating, taking their seats now, the women dressed in pastels and summer whites, their laughter and the murmur of their conversation audible even from the distance of her balcony.

She heard happiness in those voices. Still, her gaze scanned faces for evidence of that happiness, too. Nick and Caroline, Kyle and Samantha, Rafe and Allie, Mike and Julia... For a moment, she didn't see Luke and Rocky, but then she caught the couple, holding hands, ambling back from a lakeside stroll before taking their seats. Adam and Laura, Zach and Jane, Rick and Natalie, Grant and Meredith...to a stranger, undoubtedly all those names and faces would be nothing but a confusing jumble.

Not to Kate. Each of those faces was precious and dear. Each represented another generation in the Fortune family, the children of her own children, and all the hopes and promises of the future. There had been so many weddings in the past two years...but none so critical as this one, not for her.

Rebecca was the youngest and last of her own children to be married. Kate had despaired of it ever happening. Rebecca had always been the one she was afraid would never find happiness.

Kate had done everything she could think of to make the day perfect. She'd ordered the weather gods to deliver a good day. They'd obeyed. She'd hounded the caterers, rearranged the flowers, checked the table arrangements and decorations at least three times. She'd intruded on the ushers as they dressed and tied all their tux bow ties. She'd fussed with hair and cosmetics and jewelry with all the bridesmaids.

And she'd helped dress her daughter. But when she put the Belgian lace veil on Rebecca's soft russet hair, tears had welled up in her eyes. She'd stolen in here for a few minutes alone. It was a day of sentiment, a day meant for emotion, but she just needed some moments to compose herself.

She heard the sound of a door unlatching behind her. Without needing to turn around, she knew it was Sterling. She immediately calmed down when she felt his arms gently slide around her waist. She closed her eyes, leaning back against him. It had been a long time—years—since she felt the freedom to lean against anyone.

Soon she wanted to tell the family about her own wedding plans with Sterling. He blessed her cheek with an affectionate, loving kiss. Since she was seventy-one, her days of wildly athletic passion might be done, but Kate strongly suspected that they would have a memorable wedding night on their own terms. She had never expected to find someone to love, not again, not someone she could trust and share with. Not like Sterling.

"You're nervous, Kate?" He always could sense her moods.

"Not nervous, exactly. But I am a bit exasperated with the bridegroom. That Gabe! I am perfectly entitled to give my youngest daughter a wedding present," she said irritably.

"So Gabe tore up the check, did he?"

"I offered him the use of the yacht, the plane. He wouldn't take anything. And he won't tell me where they're going on their honeymoon, either."

"Imagine that."

"He gave me a hug, told me thanks, but he could take care of my daughter with no assistance. He wouldn't let me do one damn thing. I may yet knock off his block today."

Sterling only chuckled. "Seems to me that a man that proud and bullheaded is an unbeatably perfect match for Rebecca."

"Well, that's true. But I didn't make all this money to swim in it. You'd think he'd have the kindness to let me interfere just a little."

"You'll have a chance to get him back. You can spoil the grandchildren rotten, Kate. And something tells me there just might be a bun in their oven."

"You think so?" Immediately mollified, Kate looked at the groom below. Gabe had just shown up, and had taken his place, waiting for his bride. Unlike any normal groom, Gabriel failed to look the least nervous. His shoulders appeared ten feet wide in the white tux, and his manner was totally relaxed and commanding. There was a grin on his face that any mother would take exception to. Gabriel looked happier than a pirate who'd just stolen a boatload of treasure.

It gave Kate great pleasure to recall the last time she'd seen him in her office. He'd been as rattled and shook up as a frantic cougar. And she'd known, right then, that he was the ideal mate for her youngest.

She could almost forgive him for being stubborn as a goat about taking any money from her.

Sterling touched her cheek. "You've kept the secret?"

She nodded. "It's been so hard. I don't want anything to distract from Rebecca's day. But I have to admit that keeping such wonderful news quiet has taken all my willpower."

The whole family was aware that the Secret Youth Formula had been perfected...but only she and Sterling knew that it had now passed the FDA standards with flying colors. Her new brainchild was ready to be marketed.

There was a new fortune to be made, another landmark in the Fortune family dynasty, and Kate couldn't have been more excited about pursuing it.

Deliberately she touched the charm bracelet on her wrist. Just a few charms dangled there, but she knew she'd see her granddaughter—and even some of her male descendants!—wearing their own charms. It was a sign of their family. She had given the bracelet to Rebecca to wear, had sensed that her youngest had found strength in the talisman. The bracelet had always been a symbol of family, a reminder of love and loyalty and all that family could and needed to be for each other.

But Kate had taken back the keepsake this morning...and given her youngest a gold charm bracelet of her own. Rebecca needed no more reminders, no more token symbols. She was about to start her own dynasty, her own way.

Sterling touched her arm. "Are you ready to go down and give your darling away, sweetheart?"

"More than ready." She lifted her chin, and took his hand. It wouldn't do for the mother of the bride to be late.

For a brief moment, though, she considered the time in her life when nothing had seemed more important than amassing power and a fortune. Over the years, Kate had learned to define *fortune* very differently from the way she once had.

Her children had found happiness. Her family was together. And that was the only fortune that could possibly matter.

* * * * *

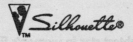

New York Times **Bestselling Author**

REBECCA BRANDEWYNE

FOR GOOD OR FOR EVIL—
THE INSIDE STORY...

The noble Hampton family, with its legacy of sin and scandal, suffers the ultimate tragedy: the ruthless murder of one of its own.

There are only two people who can unravel the case—

JAKE SERINGO is the cynical cop who grew up on the mean streets of life;

CLAIRE CONNELLY is the beautiful but aloof broadcast journalist.

They'd parted years ago on explosive terms—now they are on the trail of a bizarre and shocking family secret that could topple a dynasty.

GLORY SEEKERS

The search begins at your favorite
retail outlet in June 1997.

MIRA The brightest star in women's fiction

Silhouette

SPECIAL EDITION™

That SPECIAL *Woman!*

IT TAKES A VERY SPECIAL MAN TO WIN THAT SPECIAL WOMAN... Don't miss **THAT SPECIAL WOMAN!** every other month from some of your favorite authors!

May 1997   **HUSBAND BY THE HOUR**
                 by Susan Mallery (SE#1099)

To satisfy her family, Hannah Pace needed Nick Archer to pretend to be her husband. But this upstanding lady cop never imagined their charade would become all too real—or that the disarmingly sexy Nick was not who he seemed!

July 1997   **THE 200% WIFE**
                 by Jennifer Greene (SE#1111)

Abby Stanford gave her all to everything she tried. So when she met sexy Gar Cameron, she set out to prove she'd be the *perfect* wife. But Gar didn't want perfection...he wanted her love—200%!

September 1997   THE SECRET WIFE
                 by Susan Mallery (SE#1123)

Five years ago, Elissa's dreams were coming true when she married Cole Stephenson—but their honeymoon was short-lived. Yet, when Elissa returned to bring proper closure to her and Cole's relationship, she realized she *really* wanted a second chance. Could they rekindle their love?

New York Times Bestselling Authors

JENNIFER BLAKE
JANET DAILEY
ELIZABETH GAGE

Three *New York Times* bestselling authors bring you three very sensuous, contemporary love stories—all centered around one magical night!

It is a warm, spring night and masquerading as legendary lovers, the elite of New Orleans society have come to celebrate the twenty-fifth anniversary of the Duchaise masquerade ball. But amidst the beauty, music and revelry, some of the world's most legendary lovers are in trouble....

Come midnight at this year's Duchaise ball, passion and scandal will be...

Unmasked

Revealed at your favorite retail outlet in July 1997.

MIRA The brightest star in women's fiction

New York Times bestselling author

LINDA LAEL MILLER

Two separate worlds, denied by destiny.

THERE AND NOW

Elizabeth McCartney returns to her centuries-old family home
in search of refuge—never dreaming escape would lie over a
threshold. She is taken back one hundred years into the past and
into the bedroom of the very handsome Dr. Jonathan Fortner,
who demands an explanation from his T-shirt-clad "guest."

But Elizabeth has no *reasonable* explanation to offer.

Available in July 1997 at your favorite retail outlet.

And the Winner Is...
You!

...when you pick up these great titles
from our new promotion at your
favorite retail outlet this June!

Diana Palmer
The Case of the Mesmerizing Boss

Betty Neels
The Convenient Wife

Annette Broadrick
Irresistible

Emma Darcy
A Wedding to Remember

Rachel Lee
Lost Warriors

Marie Ferrarella
Father Goose

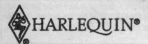 

Meet the Fortunes—a family whose legacy is greater than riches. Because where there's a will...there's a *wedding!*

FORTUNE'S Children™

If you missed any Fortune's Children titles, then order now and experience the romances of the entire Fortune family!

#50177	HIRED HUSBAND (Caroline's Story)	$4.50 U.S. ☐
	by Rebecca Brandewyne	$4.99 CAN. ☐
#50178	THE MILLIONAIRE AND THE COWGIRL	$4.50 U.S. ☐
	(Kyle's Story) by Lisa Jackson	$4.99 CAN. ☐
#50179	BEAUTY AND THE BODYGUARD	$4.50 U.S. ☐
	(Allie's Story) by Merline Lovelace	$4.99 CAN. ☐
#50180	STAND-IN BRIDE (Michael's Story)	$4.50 U.S. ☐
	by Barbara Boswell	$4.99 CAN. ☐
#50181	THE WOLF AND THE DOVE	$4.50 U.S. ☐
	(Rachel's Story) by Linda Turner	$4.99 CAN. ☐
#50182	SINGLE WITH CHILDREN	$4.50 U.S. ☐
	(Adam's Story) by Arlene James	$4.99 CAN. ☐
#50183	A HUSBAND IN TIME	$4.50 U.S. ☐
	(Jane's Story) by Maggie Shayne	$4.99 CAN. ☐
#50184	WIFE WANTED	$4.50 U.S. ☐
	(Natalie's Story) by Christine Rimmer	$4.99 CAN. ☐
#50185	MYSTERY HEIRESS	$4.50 U.S. ☐
	(Jessica's Story) by Suzanne Carey	$4.99 CAN. ☐
#50186	THE WRANGLER'S BRIDE	$4.50 U.S. ☐
	(Grant's Story) by Justine Davis	$4.99 CAN. ☐
#50187	FORGOTTEN HONEYMOON	$4.50 U.S. ☐
	(Kristina's Story) by Marie Ferrarella	$4.99 CAN. ☐
	(limited quantities available on certain titles)	

TOTAL AMOUNT	$
POSTAGE & HANDLING	$
($1.00 for one book, 50¢ for each additional)	
APPLICABLE TAXES*	$ _____
TOTAL PAYABLE	$ _____
(check or money order—please do not send cash)	

To order, send the completed form, along with a check or money order for the total above, payable to Silhouette Books, to: **In the U.S.**: 3010 Walden Avenue, P.O. Box 9077, Buffalo, NY 14269-9077; **In Canada**: P.O. Box 636, Fort Erie, Ontario, L2A 5X3.

Name: _____

Address: _____ City: _____

State/Prov.: _____ Zip/Postal Code: _____

*New York residents remit applicable sales taxes.
Canadian residents remit applicable federal and provincial taxes.
Look us up on-line at: http://www.romance.net

Silhouette®

FCBACK11